Sudden Stories

Sudden Stories

The MAMMOTH Book
of Miniscule Fiction

Edited by Dinty W. Moore

DuBois, Pennsylvania

First revised edition

ISBN: 0-9718059-5-4

MAMMOTH books
is an imprint of
MAMMOTH press inc.
7 Juniata Street
DuBois, Pennsylvania 15801

info@mammothbooks.com
www.mammothbooks.com

Cover designed by
Dinty W. Moore
and
Mary Kay Stoddard
mks107@graphic-designer.com

Associate Editor Jonathan W. Holmes

Table of Contents

THE MOMENT OF TRUTH: AN INTRODUCTION

There is a moment in the experience of reading fiction that I find irresistible, a moment where my breath catches up in my throat. It is usually the moment where I realize what the story is "about," what is really at stake for the character, what the writer has been setting into motion with carefully chosen words and details. I absolutely love that sudden recognition; it feels exactly as if a moment of communication – communion? – has occurred between myself and the writer. It is always a human moment, to my mind, almost never about language or cleverness.

This moment to which I refer resembles precisely those infrequent occasions in my *real* life when I look across the table and suddenly truly understand the person I am talking to. I understand what they are saying to me, I understand what they want to happen, and I understand what they really need – often three different things, by the way. This moment of revelation is rare in my real life, but it almost always comes in fiction, when the fiction is true.

That is why I read.

What I love about the exceptionally brief stories found in this volume, these sudden stories, is the way that they often bring me to this point of recognition in a paragraph or two, and then leave me there, absolutely suspended. There is no gentle letdown, no winding down, no expulsion of air – just that wonderful moment.

The other thing I love is that there are so many stories here, all so different, from so many authors. There is a pleasure and satisfaction in getting behind a writer's ocular openings, seeing the world through the lenses of her eyes. You can do it here, in short order, about 135 times.

So there you have it. Why I edited this book.

Since I also edit an online journal of sudden nonfiction, *BREVITY* – (www.brevitymag.com) – I am often asked to defend the brief prose form. I use the word "defend" very deliberately. Some people become truly huffy about the matter, as if the choice to use a mere two or three hundred words was an affront of some sort to those writers who choose to use ten- or twenty-thousand. Is it the gradual deterioration of our intellect, I'm asked, or is it that the pervasive use of e-mail, beepers, and text pagers, has left us with incredibly abbreviated attention spans?

I would say yes and no. The term "short attention span" has become code for stupid and shallow – the worst of MTV. To suggest that we have "short attention spans" is to suggest ignorance, and I simply don't buy that. Yes, society has changed, nearly every aspect of our lives has quickened, but that doesn't make us into a race of senseless boobs.

On the other hand, life *has* quickened, and storytelling *has* changed. A long time ago when people sat by the campfire, and not too long ago when people sat around a radio, to hear stories, there was great advantage to someone who could string a narrative out, make it last forever, fill up the night air with words. The same was true of the novel. The literate class had many, many evening hours to fill, and often filled them with long books.

Well, like it or not, that situation no longer exists. People today consume information at a much-accelerated rate. Some of the information they consume is shallow and of little value, certainly, but some is incredibly sophisticated. The best examples of short short fiction fall into the latter category, I think – though brief, they are incredibly sophisticated, stuffed to the gills.

One of the reasons I am undertaking this new anthology is that I teach introductory fiction writing classes to undergraduates nearly every semester, and sudden stories are a highly effective way to get students started. The abbreviated length allows a beginning writer to try her hand numerous times at solving the story problem, and in my opinion, the more mistakes a student makes, the more she learns. The length also undercuts a student's occasional urge to paste the 90-minute movie plot into a 10-page short story format. You just can't do that with the flash. It forces a student to re-think most of what they know about narrative. And to my way of thinking, that is a good thing.

Students of the genre should make a point of reading "What is a Sudden Story?" near the back of this book. The definitions are lively, instructive, and may lead you to write your own.

And by the way, if you *are* a student, you may be heartened to know that side-by-side with some of the well-published, award-winning authors on these pages, there are students – graduate and undergraduate. A careful reader can study the author's bio notes at the back to discern who they are, but other than that, I don't think you can tell. This pleases me.

Oh, and one last thing. The stories in this book are all 350 words or less, except a few that slipped in slightly over length. What can I say? When I read a wonderful bit of storytelling, I go weak in the knees. I lose my ability to count.

Dinty W. Moore

Acknowledgements

Many thanks go to the talented writers who graciously allowed their work to appear on these pages. Thanks as well to my associate editor Jonathan W. Holmes, to Penn State Altoona and Kenneth A. Womack for their support of this project, and to MAMMOTH books founder, publisher, editor, and limo driver Antonio Vallone, a man of great heart.

PROTEST

Molly Giles

Two girls lie on their stomachs in the middle of the road, giving the finger to every car that passes. Most cars honk but a soccer mom stops, parks her SUV, and crosses over. "What are you doing?" she asks the girls, her voice low and serious. "Don't you know you could get killed?" Her cargo of little boys stares out the windows. The girls slowly rise to their elbows, eyes blank. Both are thirteen. Both are beautiful. "Fuck you," the dark haired girl says. "Fuck you," her blonde friend echoes. A man in a pickup brakes. "What kind of language is that?" he shouts. "Fuck you," the girls say together, and put their heads back down on the asphalt. "You know what?" the man says. "You deserve to get run over." A gray haired woman with an *Earth First!* sticker on her Honda leans out and calls, "Are they protesting? What are they protesting?" "They're protesting being teenagers," another woman says as she jogs briskly by. "Drugs," an old man decides as he and his golf partner peer out the windows of their BMW. "Everything's drugs," the golf partner agrees. "Or worse." The girls roll over onto their backs, arch, stretch, look up at the sky. "Please get out of the road," the soccer mom pleads. The blonde raises her middle finger. The brunette does the same. The soccer mom walks back to her car, gets out her cell phone, and dials the police. "Don't ever grow up," she warns the little boys in the back. But it's already too late. She glances in the rear view mirror and sees her own son's gaze slide away from her as he and his teammates sit silently, breath held, eyes shining.

KASPAR SOUP

Christina Milletti

That spring, the Kaspar's lost their possessions the way trees lose their leaves in the fall. The housekeys were first to disappear. Then flashlights, receipts. After dinner, Pina's sharpest knife went missing. Ham lost his driver's license the following day. Within a week, the boys lost their books. Their backpacks were sitting beside them as the schoolbus bounced. The boys and books went up together. Only the boys came down.

Each night, Pina lay in bed waiting for things to disappear. She didn't question the losses. Instead, she gathered her precious belongings—the first lock of hair cut from Milne's scalp, Bobby's infant toenails. A stone Ham once found in the surf. His only silk tie, a typewriter key. To these she added a stack of photos which, behind shadows and thumbprints, documented her marriage. She hid the collection in a crockpot. The boys would never find it there.

"I'm making dinner," Ham said when Pina arrived from work one night. He was using the crockpot, steam rose from its rim. "The boys?" she asked. He stirred the pot, wiped his lip with his shirt. "They were gone when I came home." He began ladling soup into two bowls.

The broth was clear except for Milne's hair and Bobby's nails. Pina's photographs julienned into slivers. Ham had smashed the type key to bits, stripped his tie down to threads. Pulverized stone into a fine, edible grain.

They sipped the broth slowly. The sliced photos slipped over Pina's tongue, the type bits against her teeth. By the end of the meal, only the grain was left. Tilting the bowl over her lips, Pina let the gritty powder run down her throat. It collected low in her belly, a heap of wet sand into which her life settled, newly buried like shells at low tide.

BOUNCING

Keith Loren Carter

Standing at the kitchen sink, blinking away sleep, he hears his wife's scream "Oh God!" followed by a terrible bumping and crashing, which he knows as sure as he's standing there in his boxers is his baby son bouncing down the stairs, just as he has always feared, and he drops the coffee pot and runs to the foot of the staircase in time to catch the startled body as it tumbles off the last carpeted stair, a plastic toddler gate crashing behind and hitting—*Thock!*—the wall, leaving a big hole that could have easily been his son's perfect head, but instead he's holding that head in one hand, cradling the rest of his tense, Pooh-clad body in his arms, staring at the tiny face, contorted in a frozen, soundless scream of fear and wonder, smooth skin turning crimson, breath held for an eternity as he hears his wife's "Please God," echo his own prayers along with his voiced pleading "Breathe, Lorne," when the logjam breaks at last, tears flow and cries like someone is sticking him with a sewing needle erupt out of the suddenly heaving body, threatening to rupture his membranes, and then just as suddenly the cat strolls by, blissfully unconcerned with the drama before her, and the tortured expression of his son clears as sunny as a solstice morning, leaving only a mother and father, their lives no longer their own.

EXCUSES I HAVE ALREADY USED

Antonia Clark

He hit me first. She called me four-eyes. The dog ate it. It's not my turn. Everybody else is doing it. My alarm didn't go off. I didn't know it was due. My grandmother died. My roommate threw it in the trash. He got me drunk. He said he loved me. He said he'd pull out in time. She pulled right out in front of me. I didn't know how you felt. I was only trying to help. He backed me into a corner. It just slipped out of my hand. I was in a hurry. It was on sale. I needed a little pick-me-up. It calms my nerves. They looked too good to resist. It sounded like such a good deal. Hospitals give me the creeps. He's probably tired of visitors. He didn't even recognize me last time. There were extra expenses this month. My vote wouldn't have counted, anyway. The kids were driving me nuts. I didn't have time. My watch must have stopped. I couldn't find the instructions. Somebody else must have used it last. I forgot my checkbook. I gave at the office. I've got a headache. I've got my period. It's too hot. I'm too tired. I had to work late. I got stuck in traffic. I couldn't get away. I couldn't let them down. I didn't know how to say no. We were thrown together by circumstance. He made me feel like a woman again. I didn't know what I was doing. It seemed like a good idea at the time. I've been up to my eyeballs. The flight was delayed. My car broke down. My hard drive crashed. I've got a call waiting. I'm flat out. Life is too short. It's too late to go back.

IT WOULD'VE BEEN HOT

Melissa G. McCracken

The first and only night he and I had sex his apartment building burned down and though the "official" cause was 2B's hotplate, I wanted to blame him as I huddled in his winter coat and boxer shorts beside the fire truck—blame him because he'd been reckless and impatient, hadn't used a condom or even the couch, instead mauling me in his hallway, all long before I said, "Do you *smell* that?" and he threw open the front door, drowning us in choking smoke before he slammed it shut, coughing, and I tried to yell "back stairs" but I couldn't breathe, yet I saw him reach up with the flat of his palm and place it against the now-closed door (like in those old school-safety films) just to see, had he bothered, if it would've been hot—the same way he reached out, as the firemen pulled away, and placed his hand against the small of my back in a gesture I guess was meant to be tender but instead was after the fact.

IMPLOSION

Melissa G. McCracken

"Spontaneous combustion," he says. We're on the couch in my apartment and he is braiding, unbraiding, rebraiding my hair. I laugh. Spontaneous combustion sounds funny—calls up an image of his thin body bursting in a "poof," leaving only wispy smoke trails to drift skyward. In truth, it is probably a messy death, but I can't shake the image of him just disappearing.

He is telling me how he would like to die if he could choose. "Maybe a meteor falling on my head," he says. I think of cartoon cats crushed by space boulders that have been pulled to earth by wicked mice. The shocked look on the cats' faces just before impact always cracks me up.

I say that I want to slip away quietly in my sleep. I almost add "alone" but think better of it. I shift around on the couch, present him my feet for a massage. He says, "Front page headlines... blaze of glory... infamy."

I shake the braid from my hair, toss my head, tease him with the wordless promise of hair in his eyes, across his chest, in his mouth. "How about implosion?" I ask, which I immediately regret. I already know that he will die of a broken heart.

IN THE MIDDLE

Michael A. Arnzen

The hallway is empty, save for one teenager who approaches me. He is large, trucker-size, sweating. He wears a black T-shirt emblazoned with three words:

Sex. Murder. Art.

The words are stacked with sex on top and art on the bottom. Murder's in the middle.

He passes me by. I know he just left art class. I heard that today they would be exposed to their first nude model. But it's only 11:17—class shouldn't be over yet. Perhaps he finished early. His footsteps echo down the empty hall like the period after each word. I follow him.

WEATHERING

Gwendolyn Joyce Mintz

He didn't know any better so he wore it and just as proud as anybody, that garbage bag his mama borrowed from a neighbor, waking up to find it raining and him without a raincoat and it would always be so because there was always something else needed and anyway he'd die in his eighth year because not only didn't he own a raincoat, he didn't own a jacket and certainly not one that was bulletproof—but that day he didn't care; he was happy to be dry like everyone else.

REUNION

Susan Perabo

"4-B," my mother says. Our car idles in the long shadow of the apartment building. I imagine my father looking down from his window, his palms slick as mine.

"Meet me right here. Two hours."

"Okay."

I'm out. But the window jerks down a crack; her lips hardly move when she speaks, like she wants me to hear it without having to say it:

"Tell him hello. For me."

"Sure."

My feet are tingly-asleep, and the door to the building is so heavy it takes both arms to open. I have not seen my father in three years, but now he is *getting himself back on track*. His own phrase, from a letter my mother let lay unopened on the kitchen table for two days. When she finally sliced it loose she read it to me, every word, including the part that said it was only me he wanted to see.

There's a tiny room off the lobby that contains a floppy plant, a humming snack machine, and a gap-toothed girl. She's sitting on the floor, sorting through a plastic bag swollen with stamps, organizing them into neat piles. I approach her, thinking of my mother circling the block for one hundred and nineteen more minutes. I sit, reach for the bag.

"Purple and lavender are separate stacks," she says.

Twenty minutes later my father enters the lobby. He can't see me from where he stands, but I can see his reflection in the glass door. He looks around, frowns. I scoot behind the snack machine and the girl cuts her eyes at me. I shake my head, put my finger to my lips.

"How was it?" my mother asks when I climb into the car at the appointed time.

I tell her it was all right.

FAST FORWARD

Maurice Kilwein Guevara

I marry, I divorce, I put three quarters in a parking meter in Milwaukee, it's the next year, then the end of spring four years later, and now I'm married to the woman whose reflection I saw in the dark blue window of a classroom. We move to the foothills of the Alleghenies, to a farmhouse owned by a deaf couple. There are clouds and a blue sky, milking cows. The old man always has a hammer and a can of nails he rattles; when the windows are open you can hear him and the old woman screaming at each other. My new wife complains about the rusty water. She's thirsty and urgent, I want to make a baby too, one night I mount her on the bare kitchen floor. Three weeks later her period comes heavier than the months before. By fall, still barren, we both start to see them: The blurred Amish woman in dark bonnet by the landing, the streak of the infant in her arms, the x-ray fingers of the baby, the ghost mop luminous in the corner by the starry window.

GRIMM THE JANITOR

Maurice Kilwein Guevara

Grimm the janitor dressed in civilian clothes.

He had one arm that didn't work completely. It was withered some and scarred but it served Grimm as a rest for his mop. I helped him the summer I was seventeen scrub and wax the classrooms of the elementary school. The whole time I worked for him he said *yes* and *nope* and *warsh that* and *move it* and *poosh that there* and very little else except for the day there was a thunderstorm; then he talked nonstop for twenty-five minutes.

Grimm said: "Stay in school, boy."

Grimm said: "I ain't educated, see, but least I got eyes."

Grimm said: "Dragonflies skin the water like them helicopters in Vietnam."

Grimm said: "Don't nobody got to make you pray or pledge allegiance to nothing."

Grimm said: "I use this hand to hold the phone when I talk to the talk show man on the AM radio and eat my frozen dinner and drink my Iron City and tell him war is rich old men spilling out the blood of the young and poor."

Grimm said: "Same hand I use to steady my .22."

Grimm said: "Ever skin a rabbit in the sunshine?"

Grimm said: "One day the government come knocking on my door and says, boy, now you got to get in a plane and fly a whole day and get off and kill some people you can't even talk to. They said yunz shoot that grandma, she's a spy what lives down in the ground."

Grimm said: "Once I even stomped on a baby's head."

Grimm said: "French marigolds bring the lady bugs that eat the aphids on your tomato plants. And the aphids came here in the first place because they should have kept them Norway maples in Norway where they belong."

Grimm said: "And all them city problems started with that bussing."

Grimm said: "I read where the whole mine just flatten like a pancake."

Grimm said: "Shit."

Grimm said: "Rain stop, boy. Poosh that there."

WALLET

Allen Woodman

Tired of losing his wallet to pickpockets, my father, at seventy, makes a phony one. He stuffs the phony wallet with expired food coupons and losing Florida lottery tickets and a fortune cookie fortune that reads, "Life is the same old story told over and over."

In a full-length mirror, he tries the wallet in the back pocket of his pants. It hangs out fat with desire. "All oyster," he says to me, "no pearl."

We drive to the mall where he says he lost the last one. I am the wheelman, left behind in the car, while my father cases a department store.

He is an old man trying to act feeble and childlike, and he overdoes it like stage makeup on a community-theater actor. He has even brought a walking stick for special effect. Packages of stretch socks clumsily slip from his fingers. He bends over farther than he has bent in years to retrieve them, allowing the false billfold to rise like a dark wish and be grappled by the passing shadow of a hand.

Then the unexpected happens. The thief is chased by an attentive salesclerk. Others join in. The thief subdued, the clerk holds up the reclaimed item. "Your wallet, sir. Your wallet." As she begins opening it, searching for identification, my father runs toward an exit. The worthless articles float to the floor.

Now my father is in the car, shouting for me to drive away. There will be time enough for silence and rest. We are both stupid with smiles and he is shouting, "Drive fast, drive fast."

CHEATING POTATO

Tyson Sharbaugh

"You have to believe me. It has nothing to do with you."

"Then what does it have to do with?" Mrs. Potato Head screams from the other side of the room, holding a bra she fears belongs to Barbie.

"It's... It's..."

"I swear, if you say 'it's a guy thing' I will come right over there and slap that stupid grin off your face."

"Sorry." Mr. Potato Head glances down at his lips, reaches over to his nightstand where he keeps his accessories, and places the grin in the back of the drawer. He pauses for a moment, staring at his collection of mouths.

"YOU PUT ON A MOUTH AND SPEAK TO ME!" she screams, her voice shaking the cardboard walls.

Mr. Potato Head turns to reveal a pearly-white smile, a mouth he hasn't worn since their wedding day.

"HOW DARE YOU!" she cries, charging toward her husband. Three quick swipes and he's left with only ears to hear his hysterical wife.

"Now you listen to me," she starts. "I don't ever want to see your eyes, nose, or lips around me ever again. We are through, got it?"

He wants to respond but cannot. Instead he gives her a thumbs up.

"Now get out," she says, right before breaking down into tears.

Blind and mute, Mr. Potato Head stands up and climbs out of the box. He falls from the top and lands outside, his back making a hollow plastic sound as it hits the cold wooden floor. Lips, noses, and eyes rain down on him. He can still hear his wife crying inside the box.

His hands begin searching the floor until he grabs a mouth and places it on his face.

"I'm sorry," he whispers.

ALICE

Pam Ullman

Ambivalent about motherhood, Alice took a job as a gravedigger. It was hard finding a graveyard that preferred a skinny girl with a shovel to a hurly-burly digging machine. Most hung up when they heard her skinny girl voice; others just laughed out loud. She was lucky to find a taker in Silas Bean. "Alice O'Dea. Nineteen. One abortion," she told him. Bean understood; she was aching to bury babies. "Come back on Monday," he said.

In bed that night, her husband's whiskers raked her chin. She folded her hands beneath her cheek and slept with her eyes full open. In the morning, they were dry and small.

On Monday, Bean was waiting for her, tall and straight like the trees that lined the side of the road that autumn. The orange leaves danced upon her heart, and she plucked one from the old man's hair, the way she'd once removed an egg from a robin's nest. She followed Bean to a narrow stream; the sun bounced off the water and sprayed his beard like fairy dust. "Got a Baby Doe up the hill a piece," he told her. "Dig fast. "Pastor's coming." Alice dug hard, while a gray-blue breeze stirred the leaves of a crippled oak that stabbed at the water with a fractured arm. A quiet rain began to fall.

The pastor carried a box in a sling, like the one her husband used to haul firewood. He extended the box like a gift.

Alice covered the grave with orange leaves, took shelter from the rain beneath a tree, felt a wisp of something fine brush her cheek. Reaching up, she touched the whole of the web, its intricate patterns and fragile lines, the strange white openings and closings. Carefully, she fingered her way to the other side.

CAT CUSTODY

Richard Pearse

"This cat is mine," my wife says. "I saw him first."

"But I'm his favorite," I say, slipping him a five.

The cat, his name is Chester, gives me a wink and takes the bill off somewhere in his mouth. He is a cat the color of sunshine striking gold.

Meanwhile there are many chores to do. We sort clothes to be cleaned, trash and papers thrown out. So many years of mutual waste and filth!

Bringing down some old blankets, I find my wife hiding in a corner of the basement, stroking Chester. "What do you think you're doing, dear?"

She draws a knife and I see her plan. A good thing I brought my knife too.

While we are circling each other, there in the dark basement, I manage to reach with my other hand into my pocket and hand Chester a ten. I can assume his wink but must keep my eye on my wife.

When it is almost totally dark, her knife hand springs forward. I step aside and my knife goes in, below her ribs. I did not see her other knife, but there it quickly is, in my chest.

Lying here, her on top of me, I see Chester make his way out the cat door of the basement, with a bundle of bills in his mouth. My wife murmurs "Go, Chester. Money well spent."

So it is her bribe money as well as mine, and Chester has gained custody of himself. I am in great pain and cannot move much, pinned down with her. But I can turn my head and wink at him. "Go, Chester. Remember who your favorite is." In the dark I cannot see, but I know Chester turns and winks at me, me alone.

GOD

Pamela Painter

My friend calls and tells me there's no other way. She says she'll just come out and say it, "Grace is dead." There are two Graces in our lives. Both are women deserving of the name. My friend is crying. She says Grace was driving to work. I picture one Grace hunched forward in the cab of her pickup, her breath steaming up the window as she uses a glove to wipe the sweat from the glass. Dogs would be bounding at her door, not happy at being left behind. Her husband would haul them back and slap the fender in farewell before he went back to patching shingles that had blown off the front porch roof. I picture the other Grace throwing files and briefs into her Honda, toast with peanut butter perched next to the open sunroof. My friend says that a delivery truck skidded into her. They rushed her to the hospital and operated for six hours but she never woke up. I picture Grace's pale blonde hair dyed red with blood and spread on a white gurney, her clothes cut off, tubes and machines doing their work. Her husband weeps over her hands. There is no talking to him. Then I picture the other Grace's short black hair slicked wet with blood, her clothes cut off, tubes and machines doing their work. Her brother's head is bowed in disbelief at this ending to their petty—her words—estrangement.

There's no other way. I have to ask. I say, tell me which one, which Grace? And then—like God—she tells me.

THE NEW YEAR

Pamela Painter

It's late Christmas Eve at Spinelli's when Dominic presents us, the waitstaff, with his dumb idea of a bonus—Italian hams in casings so tight they shimmer like Gilda's gold lame stockings.

At home, Gilda's waiting up for me with a surprise of her own: my stuff from the last three months is sitting on the stoop. Arms crossed, scarlet nails tapping the white satin sleeves of her robe, she says she's heard about Fiona. I balance the ham on my hip and pack my things—CD's, weights, a vintage Polaroid—into garbage bags she's provided free of charge. Then I let it all drop and offer up the ham in both hands, cradling it as if it might have been our child. She doesn't want any explanations—or the ham.

Fiona belongs to Dominic, and we are a short sad story of one night's restaurant despair. But the story's out and for sure I don't want Dominic coming after my ham. The ham glistens beside me in the passenger seat. Somewhere in Indiana I strap it into a seat belt.

I stop to call, but Gilda hangs up every time. So I send her pictures of my trip instead: The Ham under the silver arch of St. Louis; The Ham at the Grand Canyon; The Ham in Las Vegas. I'm taking a picture of The Ham in the Pacific when a big wave washes it out to sea. I send the picture anyway: The Ham in the Pacific Undertow. In this picture, you can't tell which of us is missing.

ON DROWNING

Melanie Rae Thon

My mother swims and drowns and swims and drowns. I do nothing to stop her. These things happen forever. Blistering sun, green waves – she's not tired. She strokes toward the Island of Wild Horses, as if the horses call her. *Rina.* My sister and I gather wishing stones, smooth as eggs, dinosaur birds. Careless girls, we forget to watch. *Mother.* So we'll never know where or when we lose her. Each stone has a band of white, a seam of quartz, but not a place you can break open.

These are my hands, the lines on my palms. The black-haired woman in the carnival tent says broken lines mean bad luck. As if I need her to tell me. She leans close; she speaks slowly. The nuns say Mother is an angel. I dream of her, fins instead of wings: this mother grabs my ankles; this angel drags me to the bottom of the lake, where the temperature is always thirty-four degrees, summer and winter. Her long hair tangles around my throat. She kisses my eyelids. Nobody will find us.

Searchlights swing at dusk. Fools. Our mother who sinks in heaven laughs with her mouth full. Light does not penetrate water. Don't they know this? One by one the men return. But not our father.

The moon reflects: its silvery image shimmers and stretches. This long, bright path could bring my father back to shore where I stand waiting. I cannot call. He cannot see me. He rocks in his wooden boat, still believing Rina might rise up and want him.

A SHAVE

Josip Novakovich

I wanted to become a doctor, but I had to quit school after fourth grade to help support my younger siblings. My parents convinced me that being a barber would be almost like being a doctor- so at first, before becoming a baker, I was a barber. I learned the trade in a couple of months so that when my boss went bingeing in the taverns he's let me run the shop. It was all right until one day when my neighbor Ishtvan came along for a shave. I place a white apron around his neck, sharpen the switchblade on leather, and lather him up nicely.

Foam touches Ishtvan's hairs, which stick half an inch out of his nose, and he sneezes.

"Do you want your nose hairs cut or plucked?" I ask. He does not answer but sneezes again, blowing the foam down all over the shop.

"*Gesundheit*" I say.

Ishtvan sneezes again, for the third time. I say "To your health, neighbor Ishtvan! May you outlive many wives!" But Ishtvan does not say "Thank you!" though he is a famously polite man. Instead he keeps his hand in front of his nose. He waits for the sneeze to come up and out. After he hasn't sneezed a minute later, I say, "Should I hit your back?" As I raise my hand, his hand drops in his lap. His head nods to one side. I take a look at him and shake him, until I realize he's dead. I fetch his wife. She runs in and says, "He's going to get rid of his mustache? Is that what the fuss is about?"

"Just look at him," I say. "Don't you see? He's dead!"

The woman gasps, and shouts "Oh my God! *Wie schrecklich!*"

So I ask the lady, "What should we do? Should we carry him back?"

"Wait, what should I do, what do you say? Tell you what, why don't you finish the shave?"

"But what good will that do?"

"A lot of good," she says. "He'll need a clean shave for his wake."

She liked the shave so much that she made me promise that during the wake I'd give him two to three more shaves because the hairs of the dead grow fast.

HONEY CAKE

Josip Novakovich

See that tall house? It rests on the foundations of our old house of baked clay.

At the beginning of the war, the Germans barged in there, seized my father and grandfather from the dinner table, and shot them to death against the barn.

Several years later half a dozen Germans walked into our yard, and I had no time to run and hide in the woods, so I hid in bed and shivered under a thick goose-down cover. A pair of boots stamped over the floorboards toward me, louder and louder. The cover was pulled off and a huge soldier loomed over me. An "*Agkhh*" broke out of my throat, my eyes bulged. The German lowered his hand, I thought to strangle me. Instead, he placed his cold palm on my forehead and held it there. Then he poured a glass of water from the bucket that was on the chair in the kitchen, put some white pills into the water, crushed them with a spoon, and pressed my lips with the edge of the glass against my teeth. I could hardly swallow. The liquid was shudderingly bitter —I thought it was poison, I would keel over and die. He took a paper sack out of his black leather bag—I guess he was a military doctor—and produced a honey cake. Where he'd got it I'll never know, but I am sure he hadn't baked it himself. He gave it to me, and I have never chewed anything sweeter before or since. He looked sternly at my mouth as if to make sure I was chewing. When I finished, he handed me another, and I chewed it slowly, savoring its honey. After swallowing the last of it, I wanted more, but didn't dare ask him with my voice or my hands. My eyes shifted in the direction of the paper sack.

The German raised his forefinger and shook it sideways in front of my aching eyes, and said, "*Nein!*" That was the only word spoken between us. He stood up and walked into the yard, his boots crunching gravel, less and less. He shouted something to the soldiers, and they all marched away, raising a screen of dust.

Eh, my brother, you can't imagine how I felt right then. First he—for me it was the same German—kills my father, and then give me the sweetest cakes I could ever have!

ALTAR CALL

Steven Sherrill

When Reverend Smawley plucked his right eyeball out—the plastic one—to hold over the congregation, the church-honeys swooned. Half the backsliders, pursed-lipped and guilt-washed, like they just eked out a church-poot. The other, whooping like no tomorrow. From the edge of the sagging stage, I heard everything clear as a bell. The tent went quiet. True reverence. Anticipation. Then a soft-wet thwack as the eyeball left the socket; that was all she wrote. Oh the weeping and wailing.

Besides folding chairs and passing collection plates, I drove, and played organ. But—self-taught—by that time in the sermon, all I could do was keep up. Smawley stomping, hollering how "Jesus come down, as a piece of baling wire, and took that eye." When medical science filled up the hole with a worthless bauble, Jesus came back. Blessed him with *special* sight. "Come on! Look in this hole! See for yourself!"

Every night, his good eye patched, he gave the call. Sinners spilled into the aisles ready for miracles, even meager ones. Grocery lists, government cards, testimonials and prayer requests, offered up to that empty socket. Smawley read them all. "Go home," he'd say. "Take them little red panties off and burn them. B'leve on the Lord." "Turn away from that bottle," he'd say. "Towards Calvary."

I looked in the hole one time. We'd stopped for gas. I came out with two cans of beer. A bag of pork rinds. Set them on the roof of the Plymouth while I pumped. The Reverend, wore slap out from doing the Lord's work, clutching his thick bible, slept. Head laid against the window. That eye—open—gaped heavenward. I knelt on the oil-stained pavement, pressed my nose to the glass. I looked into that hole. I seen it all. You better believe it.

DAN QUAYLE THINKING:
ON SNIPE HUNTING

Michael Martone

They told me to wait, so I wait. They gave me a burlap sack and pushed me out of the car into the ditch next to a field. I watched the taillights disappear. They told me they would drive the snipes my way. "Wait here." And I do.

Stars are in the sky. I'm in a mint field. The branches of the low bushes brush against my legs, releasing the reeking smell.

I think, suddenly, they are not coming back. Back home, they are waiting for me to figure out they are not coming back. They are thinking of this moment, the one happening now, when I think this thought, that they are not coming back, and then come home on my own.

But, I think, I'll wait. While waiting, I'll think of them waiting for me to return home with the empty burlap sack. They'll think that I haven't thought, yet, that I was left here in the mint field, that I am waiting for them to drive the snipes my way. I'll let them think that.

In the morning, I'll be here, waiting. They will come back looking for me. Dew will have collected on the mint bushes. The stars will be there but will be invisible. And I won't have thought that thought yet, the one they wanted me to think.

The imaginary quarry is still real and still being driven my way.

MINERS

Michael Martone

Going east, I cross the Ohio by a bridge that empties on the west side smack into a mountain face tunneled through to Wheeling. Set back from the highway on the old roadbeds are the miners' houses. Mountains are at their backdoors. The highway cuts through the mountains, and on the sheer faces of the cliffs on both sides, I see where they've bored and set the charges like a pencil split in two and the lead removed.

I think about the products of coal. The stockings you wear. The records you play. The aspirin you take. The pencil you write with. These are mine. What would we do without all this carbon?

As I move, the face of the land is changing. I am going east so I can write to you.

The hillsides are quarries mining men. The men are going home where they will discover that all the waters in Shakespeare will not make them clean. This life has gotten under their skins. They make love in smudges.

I am going further east where men are inside of things, where they own things inside and out.

I am writing this with a pencil painted yellow and printed with a silhouette of a women with no arms.

I wish I were a miner so that when you turned your back to me and the face of the land changed, before I would go back underground, I would reach out and write with my black finger some graphite text on the places you could not reach.

"You," it would say, "are mine."

TIME MACHINE

Robin Hemley

I never doubted for a moment the machine would work. Desire and imagination were my engines; I assumed reality would step meekly forward and bow to my wishes. Ann Holmes, the most distant and therefore prettiest girl in the class, stepped into the box and I shut her in, then tweaked Styrofoam knobs.

After a few seconds, Anne said, "I'm still here," and I said, "No you're not."

We might have had one of those typical yes-I-am-no-you're-not exchanges if not for my art teacher who, seeing a teachable moment, wanted to grab it and wring its neck.

"What can we learn from this class?" Mrs. Dominic asked.

Tony Turnbull raised his hand urgently. "Don't tell lies."

I stepped into the time machine next. I refused to give in to either my classmate's ridicule or my teacher's reason, though clearly I was the only person who believed the time machine might still work.

When my teacher said, "It's time to come out now, Robin," I didn't. I stayed. My teacher swung open the makeshift door and saw me huddled in the little box, though I willed myself invisible. "It's time to come out now," she said again. Why she didn't leave me there, I don't know. Eventually, I would have come out. I would have pretended none of this had happened because even third graders know how to save face when it really counts. Tony Turnbull would have remarked on it, no doubt, a few sharp jabs of ridicule and then it would have been over. But Mrs. Dominic determined to make an example of me, wouldn't let it go. She yanked me out of the box, and I sat limp, silent, refusing to obey that I stay in her time, in her art class. That seemed the most important thing in the world to her at that moment, April, 1967.

THE BEGINNING OF THE STORY

Todd Davis

In the movie that the teacher shows our fourth-grade class, the small Indian boy goes into the forest in the fall of the year to select a piece of wood—perhaps the limb of a cedar, its green smell bringing the rotting leaves that line the floor alive. He carries it to his home high in the mountains where he sits before a fire, carves lines in the wood until the frame of a man emerges— paddle fixed upon his lap as he waits for the currents to pull his canoe toward open water. The camera catches the boy's prominent nose, reminds me of the commercial that runs each afternoon between Bugs Bunny and Daffy Duck cartoons: Indian Chief standing near a garbage dump; a tear rolling down the creased skin of his cheek. In the movie, snow falls with a silence that seems safe, a heaven for Mohican or Anishnabe. Then the next frame brings spring. First day when water drips from the roof. Reflected sunlight caught like dust in the projector's beam. Rivulets form in snow, gray boulders take shape, and the boy again walks into the forest where beneath hemlock boughs he places his boat. The best part of the movie now begins for the rest of the kids. Canoe washes down the mountain into rivers below, makes its way to a city harbor enclosed by buildings so tall that they cast shadows over the water that stretches outward, as if it has no end. When the lights come up in our classroom, fluorescence upon varnished hardwood floors, I wish for the movie's mountains, to run after deer with the Indian boy, a friend I will never betray, both of us happy to be nowhere near a city or its dumps, nowhere near a sea, instead always somewhere near the beginning of the story.

BLUE

Brian Doyle

One time in 1944 we were on our gunboats and discovered our compasses didn't work. Compasses then were built so the needle floated on a little sea of alcohol. Blue had opened each one and drank the juice and put them back together dry.

Get Blue over here, says the lieutenant.

Blue gets hustled over. He's drunk.

Bristol, says the lieutenant. You drank the juice from the compasses.

Yes, sir, says Blue.

Putting the regiment in danger.

Yes, sir.

That's a crime, Bristol.

There's no sound except the lap lap lap of the little waves against the boats.

I should shoot you in the head, Bristol, says the lieutenant.

Blue smiles, a little confused and a lot drunk.

Tie him to the gunwale, head down, says the lieutenant.

Sir? says Mahon.

He can drink all he wants that way, says the lieutenant.

We tie him down. Blue's sobering a little now but he's not sober enough to fight back and he hangs over the side like a dead dog.

Hey, you guys, says Blue faintly.

Back to base, says the lieutenant.

He'll drown, says Mahon quietly.

That's the idea, Mahon.

That's murder, sir, says Mahon.

People die, Mahon, says the lieutenant.

If you stop you go to jail, says the lieutenant to me.

Yes, sir.

Back to base, he says.

We take off. Blue was yelling but the little waves were gagging him. I could hear the lap lap lap from where I sat and the sound he made when he tried to catch his breath between the waves.

After a minute I reached down quick and loosened the knot and Blue fell in. His feet banged the gunwale. We were near an

island and the water was maybe twenty feet deep. I took off fast.
Maybe he made it.

THE MULTIPLICATION OF WOOL

Scott Russell Sanders

Encrusted with twigs and cockleburs, the sheep drifted by her door like a filthy tide. Mrs. Josiah Ward watched the drove pass, imagining each animal a walking blanket, a four-legged shirt. "How much you want for the sheep?" she asked the drover. Glancing at the rickety cabin, the man answered, "More than you've got."

She hurried indoors, then returned blinking into the daylight. "I have a stocking here," she said. At sight of the lumpy sock dangling from her fist the drover stopped his herd. "These here sheep are bespoke by Timothy Culver," he told her, eyeing the sockful of money. "He'll only let them eat poisonweed down by the creek and kill themselves like he did the last ones," she said, taking from the stocking a handful of coins which she had brought with her from Connecticut for the single purpose of buying sheep. The deal was swiftly made, and she owned eight of the ragamuffin beasts.

That night, while the sheep mulled about in a log pen, she sheared them all in her dreams. Come morning, she found two of them slaughtered by wolves. She gathered the wool that had been strewn about the carcasses, washed out the cockleburs and blood, carded and spun it. She would weave it later into cloth for breeches. Every night afterward she locked the surviving sheep in her kitchen, where the three older children slept.

Despite her care, one of the sheep ate poisonweed, swelled up and burst. She salvaged that fleece, as well as the fleece from two others which had broken through ice on the creek. Of the three sheep still alive in the spring, only one was a dam. But she bore young, which in due time bore their own young, until Mrs. Ward owned an entire flock, all sprung from that stocking full of Connecticut coins. Her wheel spun through the day, her loom clacked into the night. Her family dressed warmly.

LOVE-CROSSED CARPENTER

Scott Russell Sanders

If you wanted carpentry work done in that part of the Ohio Valley, you hired Nathan Muzzy. He was the best man with wood in the territory, but he refused all payment for his labors except bed and board. While he fashioned wainscot for the parlor or a banister for the stair, you had to listen to him tell about his misfortunes in love.

Everyone heard the same story, which he elaborated by the hour as wood shavings flew. He had graduated from Yale College, which was a rare enough feat. Even more rare, as a young minister he had received the gift of tongues, speaking to crowd of thousands in the towns back east. Then one night at a camp meeting while he addressed the multitudes, his gaze lit upon the face of a woman in the audience, and he could not look away. He could speak to no one but her. The crowd shuffled out grumbling before he finished his sermon, and that was the end of his career as a preacher.

He followed the woman home to her father's place. She would have nothing to do with him until he proved his love by building her a house. When the dwelling was finished she demanded furniture. And when Muzzy had turned the last spindle of the last chair, she married a New Haven lawyer, with whom she moved into the bridal house.

From that day forward Muzzy had meandered westerly, raising a cabin here or a barn there, paneling a room, carving children's toys. In every lodging he retold his story. By the time he reached Ohio he was in rags and his spine was bent. The only sturdy things about him were the hands and voice.

No one could persuade him to take money, or to linger after his work was done. Between jobs he ate berries. People told of overhearing him in the woods recounting his woes in the same entranced voice—and in the same words—as he had used in their parlors.

When he was found frozen one December near the pond that was later named after him, his body a rack of bones, the local people buried him. On his last carpentry job Muzzy had been overheard to sing out, "God be praised, the Devil's raised, the world rolls round in water." What he meant by that, no one knew.

AURORA

Ronder Thomas Young

Pamela Tucker is seven years old when she falls in love with her cousin Clayton. She's never taken particular notice of him before, but when her daddy holds her up over the open casket, there's not much choice. Blond lashes curl out of his delicate eyelids. Pamela's own eyes fill up with tears. Not because he's dead, but because he's so beautiful.

Clayton is seventeen years old when he drowns in the pond behind Aunt Helena's house. He slices silently through Pamela's watery dreams.

Five years later Pamela sees John Lennon on the Ed Sullivan Show. Funny. Sad. And—just a little bit—mean. She closes her eyes, plays piano and sings a full octave lower than she can really get her voice to go. Her song is so wicked, hard and dead-on that John just cannot believe it. Pamela can never recapture the words in the morning, but she knows she's got the wicked, hard, dead-on feelings to make it happen.

Ed from work. Red hair. Flaming beard. White, white teeth. Radiates bright hot like the sun. Pamela stands with the other waitresses and watches two repo guys commandeer Ed's lime-green car out of the parking lot. Ed strolls out of the kitchen. Kisses the top of Pamela's head. Takes off his apron. Walks. Down the hill. Along the highway. Keeps walking. Never even picks up his last check.

Pamela is seventeen years old. Same as Clayton.

THIS NEW QUIET

Debra Marquart

The day after the fire, all their equipment charred in a ditch and blown to ashes, the thin axle of the truck lying on its side like the burnt-out frame of a dragonfly, they gathered in a living room on a circle of old couches. Most of them sat forward, their eyes studying the swirls in the worn carpet.

They who had the power to make so much noise sat in this new quiet. They did not speak of debt or creditors, nor did they speak of lost guitars—the blond Les Paul, and the mahogany Gibson double-neck that sang sweetly in its velvet case as it rolled down the highway.

They sat in silence, trying to find the new words the fire had left on their tongues. Outside traffic rushed by, the clatter of passing trains, the honk of angry horns, as the sun dialed its way around the room.

Finally, someone stood. It was the tall blond guitar player who rose, wobbly in his black boots. He stood in the center of the spiral, raised his thin hands to his face and blew out one long exhale. It hissed through the room like a wild balloon losing steam.

When all the wind was out of him, he gulped one deep breath, swung a long arm like a knockout punch through the emptiness of air, and said, *Fuck*. It was only one word. It was inadequate for the moment. But it was a good place to start.

DYLAN'S LOST YEARS

Debra Marquart

Somewhere between Hibbing and New York, the red rust streets of the Iron Range and the shipping yards of the Atlantic, somewhere between Zimmerman and Dylan was a pit stop in Fargo, a superman-in-the-phone-booth interlude, recalled by no one but the Danforth Brothers, who hired the young musician, fresh in town with his beat-up six string and his small town twang, to play shake, rattle, and roll, to play good golly, along with Wayne on the keys and Dirk on the bass, two musical brothers whom you might still find playing the baby grand, happy hours at the southside Holiday Inn.

And if you slip the snifter a five, Wayne might talk between how high the moon, and embraceable you, about Dylan's lost years, about the Elvis sneer, the James Dean leather collar pulled tight around his neck, about the late night motorcycle rides, kicking over the city's garbage cans, and how they finally had to let him go, seeing how he was more trouble than he was worth, and with everyone in full agreement that the new boy just could not sing.

THE DHARMA OF PUNK

Gerry LaFemina

Laura shaved the sides of Barbie's head and dyed the remaining hair red; she made a mini skirt from an old inner tube, a matching latex bustier, and painted the doll's pink heels black. Poor Ken, with plastic hair, couldn't be helped. He became another jock at school who taunted punk Barbie. This we knew.

We knew, too, the lyrics in ninety-second songs, mouthed them quicksilver as we climbed stages then leapt before bouncers struck, our arms outstretched. This was a moment— hands on our bodies passing us above spikes of blue hair. The *satori* of adrenalin. We relearned community, even as outside the skinheads chose sides....

Once she called while my mother led meditation in the living room— seven women chanting *ohm*: an electric hum. How could I explain?

We didn't mock the Trekkies we'd see on the subways wearing Spock ears, with their phasers and tricorders, heading for a TrekCon somewhere midtown. Once a group of them gawked as she buzzed my hair back into a mohawk before they continued toward their vision of the future. When she stroked the new bald above my ears, I became aware of each nerve in skin I'd forgotten.

She finally saved Ken with a bandanna and combat boots stolen from GI Joe. She added, later, a t-shirt decorated by red and black markers.

At night we'd kiss. I'd walk the quarter-mile home, unraveling all I'd learned and forgetting quiet breaths. I'd sit fake lotus, but my pulse had its own guitar and drums, incessant and loud, which nobody else could hear. I'd lie awake, that rhythm rattling my bed, and knew there was nothing I could do— knew it was desire causing this misery. Right then, I envied those dolls: their plasticine smiles, their proximity to her.

BROKE

Aimee Bender

He met a woman with eyes so black they woke up the nocturnal mammals. If you looked close enough—if she let you —if you were her lover and lucky enough to see in that intently— you could, on a summer night, find Orion near her left pupil. The great hunter. Watch out. Those seven little dots glittering, scattered on the iris, were like brands of longing on the heart of the looker, and she never left a man complete. For the rest of their lives, memories of the slippery line of her back would flit into their minds, while driving through traffic, while frying bacon, while washing sand from their childs' hands after a long reddening day at the beach. Look into the sky on a dark summer night, and there, huge, is the eye of the woman you once loved like a rocket. Try to survive that.

FIRST LOVE AND LOSS

Philip Terman

She didn't invite anyone over because the house she was growing up in was a wreck, broken down, never put back together: stale bread, fungus and rotten vegetables, dust and the unwashed odors of human flesh—scattered shells and peals, something sour, crayon scrawls on the walls, static from the t.v, ripped shades. Save for her room, immaculate and ordered, the clean wooden dresser and organized records and books, her jewelry cases and framed photographs of friends: ink drawings of roses and birds. I learned all of this later, about the numbers on her father's wrists, her mother's visits to the institutions.

Fourteen, she'd wait on the tree lawn and I drove her away: anywhere, she'd plead, dark eyes, olive skin, black hair she wouldn't cut for anything. Like a gypsy's, I thought, something about the certainty of her stare, as if something about me was special, a dazzle in the way she'd touch me lightly that made me dizzy and want—I didn't know what.

We'd whisper on the phone all night, her voice soft and desperate, until the streetlights snapped off and we'd skip school and sit beside Euclid Creek, the water blazing stones in the April light, filtering through recent buds. She showed me how to put first one then two then three fingers inside of her and how to circle them slowly, then faster, her face turning the pink the sun looks when the sky opens out.

How could I not think of her, that late afternoon, lights off in the classroom, dust swirling imperfect circles in the beam of the projector, bodies piling into a gigantic hole in the ground? Her way, I understand now, was to escape into pleasure. I wasn't a quick study. I had to learn the rest on my own.

ROCKET SCIENCE

Wendy Ring

Blast-off. After the long July of 1962 and her stay at the facility, my mother becomes caught up in the space race. Glad for her interest in something other than sadness, my park ranger father brings home left-behind newspapers from the Casa Grande Visitors' Center. She cuts out articles about cosmonauts and astronauts, pictures of Cape Canaveral and the Atlantic Ocean. Taping the stories to the walls of our government house, she almost smiles. But sometimes she puts on her best Sunday dress and sits all day in the closet.

First stage. I'm eleven. I start reading library books on Chinese fireworks and physicist Robert Goddard. One afternoon I tell my mother my theory of building a desert space center to take advantage of the dry air and slightly higher altitude, which reduce the forces of friction. With a rake she helps me clear creosote bushes and rocks, making a launch pad in the dry wash near where we live. Her hands still tremble.

Second stage. At the Visitors' Center, I tell my father I'll empty the bullet-shaped trash container. Instead I sneak it down the path to our house. "Clever boy," my mother says of our trashcan rocket rigged inside with a Mason jar of gas. She begins the countdown. I light the jump rope fuse. The flame scampers like a spider to a hole I punched in the bottom of the container. "Three," she says as a fountain of fire sends our spaceship tumbling toward mission control and us in aluminum lawn chairs.

Re-entry. We run down the wash. Behind us more than twenty acres of National Park Service land burns to lunar gray ash. But all the trouble that follows is worth it just to know my mother's laugh can return—its echo lowers gently as if borne on parachutes through the smoky sky.

BAD DOG

Jennifer Cande

It was a side-of-the-road dog. Seemed to Renee the kind of dog that someone couldn't afford to feed or that someone, drunk, kicked around. "Must've followed me here," she said. "Will you let her stay?" Ben, her husband, knelt next to the dog and smiled as Renee noticed that their tulips were wilting again. Too much water and attention Ben gave them. "Over-tending," Renee called it.

Ben threw a stick for the dog to catch and said "I haven't had a dog since 1982," when he and his brother were followed home by a stray. Their dog, Jeepers, was hit by a car not more than a week after they convinced their father to allow them to keep her. "Sometimes, in dreams, Jeepers still follows me," Ben said.

Renee watched Ben rub the dog's stomach. The word crossed her mind: Loyalty. From where she stood, plucking flimsy, rotting stems from the earth, she felt like a destroyer of all that is good and just in Ben's world.

MIRACLES

Nin Andrews

It was Indian summer, after the change in weather brought all the bees inside, when Grandma moved in. Jimmy, the farmhand, and I were sitting by the silo waiting for the milk truck when she stepped out of a yellow cab wearing a fur muff and a red satin cap. That afternoon when the sun burned through the mist, bees were crawling up the windows looking for holes in the screens. Before my mom could get a grip on her, Grandma had hosed every bug in our house down with Raid and taken over doing the laundry too. If there was a thing Grandma liked, it was clean clothes. And other things were dead bugs and the Lord, Jesus Christ. But she didn't want to be bothered with the clothes dryer. She liked our clothes hung outside, saying the Lord liked honest work which meant something you did without a socket.

It rained so much that fall, all our lettuce got slugs and the wilt. My mom said the sheets mildewed. After my grandma took the linens in from the line, they were damp and crawling with daddy long legs. Mom would slip them in the dryer, whining under her breath about how Grandma had her ways of dipping into everybody's affairs like a pumpkin vine in compost.

Nights, while Grandma read me her favorite parts of the Bible, mostly about Jesus performing the miracles, I'd sweep my sheets with my fingers, feeling for bug legs. I never could figure how any insect could walk on those legs, thin and wispy as hairs.

AS I SEE IT, YES

Rita Ciresi

My psychic adviser hung my down coat on the rack. I knew she wasn't a psychiatrist—or a priest—but I kept waiting for her to say, in a reassuring tone, *Tell me why you are here. Hormones* was hardly an intelligent answer. *Love* was even dumber. Still stupider: *the weather.* I could point to no single reason why superstition suddenly had seized me in its inane grip. I only knew that last week—whacked out on estrogens—I had sunk to new intellectual lows by asking the Magic 8-Ball if my marriage was going to survive this endless winter and had felt myself grow faint with fear when the answer bobbed up: BETTER NOT TELL YOU NOW.

Then: CANNOT PREDICT AT THIS TIME.

Then: ASK AGAIN LATER.

RUMFORD

Dinty W. Moore

Given how Uncle Skitch drank, no one in the family wanted to believe him when he insisted that Rumford could speak.

No one wanted Skitch to drive, either, but he did.

In the mornings, still stung from the four or five tumblers of whiskey he downed at the kitchen table the night before while shouting at the voices on his radio, Skitch would stumble out his front door, fumble into his massive, gray 1962 Buick—"the battleship"—and jerk-stop, jerk-stop, jerk-stop the damn car all the way to the end of the block before realizing his emergency brake was still engaged. He did this repeatedly, refusing to learn. The noise horrified everyone.

But old Skitch jerk-stopped his battleship to its final mooring spot when the railroad finally let him go. Skitch used to ride in the back of the train, watching out for equipment failure. After he lost the job, he just drank around the clock, and never drove anywhere. The neighbors were more relieved than annoyed to see that old Buick rotting out front.

Skitch still bragged about Rumford, though.

If you called Skitch at home, the dog would answer the phone. Or that is what Skitch said, anyway. Most of us thought it was his wife, Ethel. She had a deep voice from all those years of chain-smoking unfiltered Pall Malls. She loved a good practical joke.

Three years later, Skitch and Ethel vanished. The Buick disappeared from the curb. Mail piled up. The phone wasn't answered. My father finally broke into the house to find no one at home, no note, but all the clothes missing.

Police quizzed the only witness.

Rumford didn't say a thing.

ENCORE

Aimee LaBrie

In fifth grade, Philip Knight asked me to go with him, presenting a greenish gold bracelet to me. When we broke up, he threw rocks at my bike. Bobby Dittmer wore blue All-Stars and played keyboard in a Christian rock band. I made him take the Lord's name in vain. The drama major read me a Native American prayer. Later, he stopped my hand, saying, *Why are you in such a rush?* Patrick was the married Irish cook who declared my snow boots "dead cute." We ate popcorn by the handfuls and watched a black and white movie. He said, *This isn't what I thought it would be like.* Then it was. I woke up with a splinter in my back. Dan used the word "shrink," whistled Frank Sinatra songs and carried a paperback by Dostoevsky in his jeans pocket. I didn't like him, but he knew how to push forward while on top. Jack Youngblood wanted to hit me but didn't. The French guy poured Kahlua on my thighs and whispered, *Let us concentrate on the legs.* The bad poet was tortured because nothing tragic had ever happened to him. Crunchy Face told me I didn't like nature enough. We watched as I stepped on an ant. Tattoo Tom wanted me to use my teeth. I traced the green and black serpent winding around his arm. Did this hurt? *No,* he said. *None of them did.*

STE. FRANCOISE des CROISSANTS

Lola Haskins

When Françoise was small, she would run her index finger across the mound of butter that sat like a pretty hill on the plain of its wire shelf, finish with the tip, then suck at what remained under her nail. As she grew, she put aside such childish assaults on the larder and began instead to smear her bread heavily back and forth until she got bored, after which she'd lick her knife to a shine. In this way the years passed, years in which she acquired breasts and long hair black as poppy seed. Then, on the morning of her eighteenth birthday, she went into the kitchen, with no more thought than wondering whether there were hard rolls for breakfast or they had eaten them all for dinner, and there, kneeling before her, was a long-haired figure in a chef's cap. When she saw the shaft of light falling from her nonexistent window onto his faint blonde moustache, she knew that he had come from God.

Mademoiselle, said the apparition, and Françoise's mouth began immediately to water. *Oui* seeped from her shiny lips. *You love the butter, mademoiselle. N'est-ce pas?* And again, though she knew that to love butter too much was a sin, *oui* escaped Françoise. *And the bread?* It said from beneath the moustache. *You love the bread? Oui.* By now, Françoise was shivering.

Eh bien, said the angel, whose hands were white not because he was a northern angel (though he was), nor because miraculous light was shining on them (which of course it was), but because of the flour. And then he beckoned to Françoise, who had taken a shaky step towards the door. *Venez ici,* he said —and produced a plump ball of dough from the pocket of his robe. A male and godly heat came from his direction. Françoise fainted. When she woke, her visitor was gone, and in his place she found twelve crescent moons, aglow in the oven's black sky.

THE FRUIT DETECTIVE

Lola Haskins

On the table, there are traces of orange blood. There is also a straight mark, probably made by some kind of knife. The detective suspects that by now the orange has been sectioned, but there is always hope until you're sure. He takes samples. Valencia. This year's crop. Dum-de-dum-dum

The detective puts out an APB. Someone with a grudge against fruit. Suspect is armed and should be considered dangerous. He cruises the orchards. Nothing turns up except a few bruised individuals, probably died of falls.

A week passes. There are front-page pictures of the orange. No one has seen it. They try putting up posters around town. Still nothing. The detective's phone rings. *Yes*, he says. And *Yes, thanks. I'll be right over.* Another orange. This time they find the peel. It was brutally torn and tossed in a wastebasket. Probably never knew what hit it, says the detective, looking sadly at the remains.

There is a third killing and a fourth. People are taking fresh looks at their neighbors. They are keeping their oranges indoors. There is fear about, that with oranges off the streets the killer may turn to apples or bananas. The detective needs a breakthrough. He gets it. The phone rings. *If you want to know who killed the oranges, come to the phone booth at the corner of 4th and Market. Twenty minutes,* the voice says.

The detective hurries on his coat. When he gets to the booth, the phone is already ringing. It is the egg. *I did it,* says the egg, *and I'll do it again.* The detective is not surprised. No one else could have been so hard-boiled.

BABYSITTER

Anne Panning

The Kizbells give you a call. For Saturday night. You have no plans; you say yes. It's summer and you're fourteen years old in the middle of it. But what about the boyfriend? You give him a call. He's older; he knows. You get ready.

This is the Baptist minister's house. The children are bathing when you get there. Two boys with shaved heads. Pajamas then books, the parents say. They leave. A Bible study group. You watch out the window as they drive away. You look in cupboards. Nothing good. All fiber and brown bananas. Upstairs, you try to listen to the kids tell you stories about animals: andthen andthen andthen! You drown them out. The boyfriend calls. Not yet, you say. They're still up.

After pressing the kids into cool sheets, you head to the basement. The TV is there. It's damp, chilly. The boyfriend knocks at the back door and comes down. On the couch he kisses you with hands. But you jump: kidsparentsthedoor. You never give all the way. But your pants tangle by the feet, your cheeks red. You hear something pounding. The boyfriend says: shh, just let me. You consider.

Then the car in the driveway. Two doors slam in rhythm. The key in the lock, twisting. The boyfriend leaps around like fire patches land. You fastforward yourself. Ascend. Never do hook up the bra under your shirt. The boyfriend leaves. You talk it through. We don't like this at all, they say. We never gave permission. You stand guiltheavy. A big dirty child in your sneakers. They press a few bills in your palm, shake their heads. You will walk home, you tell them. It's not far.

Outside, the boyfriend waits by a pine tree. You proceed slowly. My car keys are in there, he says. They must have fallen out. You both look at the house. The boyfriend's car locked. You lean against the door, your hands behind your back, and wait for help.

YES, YES

Geoff Schmidt

There were slugs on the tree trunks in our yard.

Father came out. He handed me a bag of salt.

Sprinkle this on their backs, he said. He lit a cigarette. Mother watched from inside. He went inside.

They writhed on the rough bark. I went around the house.

I threw salt at the car. It deflated.

I threw salt at our house. It hissed away. My parents were pale on their bed.

I sat cross-legged with my salt and watched them. They clutched beneath the blue blue sky and watched me.

The wind said yes yes to the leaves.

SO YOU THINK YOU'RE SMART

Lee Martin

"Where are my specs?" my mother asks me. "Junior, I can't find my cheaters."

I tell her they're here on her dresser, right where she left them when she went down to the dining room for supper. This is what I do. I explain things. I stay patient.

"I knew that." The glasses rest on her book of brain teasers, *So You Think You're Smart*. "I just forgot. I expect you'll say it's the what's-a-hootchie, that Al Heimers. Well, mister, I don't have Al Heimers. I knew where I left my glasses. I just didn't dwell on it."

What she does dwell on is the notion she has that I'm stealing everything she's got. "Cabbaged on to my car," she tells people. "Hoodwinked me out of my house. Locked me up in the looney bin." She has a standard spiel. "I wasn't having any trouble on my own. I paid my bills. I kept my house spick and span. I was happy there. Very happy."

Very happy, she says in a small, pouty voice, and my heart breaks.

"Those aren't mine." She picks up her glasses and studies them. "No, mine have more brown in the frames."

"Those are yours," I tell her.

"Nope. Those belong to someone else." She snatches my glasses off my face. "Here, let me see these."

The answers to her brain teasers are encrypted—written backwards, slantwise, upside down, legible only when held to a mirror.

I can make out her shape, but not her features. This is only the beginning, I tell myself. I touch her lips, trace her coy grin.

Now, we're whispering.

"Give me my glasses. Please, Mother. I'm blind."

"Hold your horses, wise guy. I'll get to the bottom of this."

THE NIGHT ALIENS IN A WHITE VAN KIDNAPPED MY TEENAGE SON NEAR THE BAPTIST CHURCH PARKING LOT

Lorraine Lopez

He admits being peeved, my boy does. Not allowed to sleep over with a shady friend with no phone, only a beeper, my son settles, enough to go to bed, earlier than usual even. But he tosses, twists—then pops the screen and leaps out, scrambling for the damp lap of grass near the Baptist church parking lot across the street. In the muzzy mosquito haze funneling from the street light, he considers *in-* words, like "injustice" and "inalienable rights," when extraterrestrials—two or twenty, he can't be sure—careen in a white Dodge van—brakes shrieking, tires thumping speed bumps—onto the church lot.

Laughing and scratching like their skins don't fit, they ask for directions to Peanut's Red Neck Bar-be-que, and my boy, ever helpful, starts to explain as they hurtle from the van, rushing him. They snatch him with long, spongy arms and slam him in the back. Then, tires wailing, they haul out to the street. Cramped between crates, he's still keen to idea. When the aliens brake for a red light, he yanks the latch, spills out the rear door, runs like fire for the back streets. In an alley, he pulls a mangled girl's bike from a trash heap and wobbles home.

Because I'd locked his window after finding his bed empty, the buzzing doorbell jolts me alert. Shaken, he can barely speak. Says if I call the police, they'll *never* believe it. Shush, I say, hush. I run him a bubbling tub, press two baby aspirin into his palm, and finally tuck him to sleep. Now *I* twist and toss, pull the curtains apart to check for white vans, listen for the squeal of brakes, the awful laughter, *something* alien out there, ready to wrench my boy from me.

GIRL

Peter Markus

We were naked. Us brothers, we were naked beneath our clothes. We were naked but I knew neither one of us would say so. So I went ahead and I said what I always said. What I said was, Hey Girl. I liked that word G-I-R-L. I liked to call Girl, Girl. Girl, I said. Girl, I wish I knew what to do with my dirty boy hands. My hands, I knew, were hands that smelled of wet baseball gloved leather and wormy fishing dirt. Hold up your hands, Girl said. Like this. Girl held up her hands, fingered tips up, her narrow girl palms facing my squared off boy face. I held up my hands. As if I was saying, I give up. Now what? was what I said. Girl leaned her body in close enough to touch. She lowered her hands. Girl's hands fell down to cup and huddle round her curved by the river hips. Now close your eyes, Girl said. Then: Don't open them until I tell you. There was this light hovering just outside the edges of darkness hiding out behind the lids of my eyes. I tried but I could not make out Girl's face hiding anywhere nearby. It was like I was being held under-water. Good, Girl said. I could hear the river lisping in my ears. It wasn't saying any thing except for what it always said. What it always said was, Be boy. I knew right then I was in that place where I had always wanted to be. It was like walking on water. Or like talking to the face of Girl. Okay, Girl said. Now open your eyes. I could feel Girl's heart hammering away inside her chest. I could see it beating, too. Girl's heart wasn't shaped like a heart. It was shaped like girl: like the word, girl. Like the word, girl, scrawled in mud. Like the way the word, girl, was meant to be spelled: with twelve r's, thirteen u's, and twenty thousand l's at the end of girl, stretching across the earth.

GIRL IS A RIVER

Peter Markus

We watch Girl walk out into the river. She walks out into the river and she stops walking out when the river reaches up to her knees. Her knees are too lovely to be covered up. We call out stop at that exact moment that she herself stops her walking out. We say stop, and thank you, and wipe our hands across our brows. Girl stops and splashes some of this muddy water underneath her arms, over her head, neck and breasts. Her skin is a shining apple newly shucked of its skin. Us brothers must watch our selves from wanting too much to take a bite out of Girl. Girl is muck naked though it seems that this is a thing only us brothers see. A tug boat manned by a crew of menny men slugs on by, up river, through the legs of Girl, though they don't even toot a whistle or horn. Hard hats laid off from the mill fish for catfish with the blood of lopped off fingers, eyes locked on the stuck in the mud fishing poles, little copper bells clipped to the tips. Ring, ring, us brothers call out. The fisher men grab hold of their fishing man poles. The men on board the tug turn towards the sound of our voices. Open your eyes, we holler. Look right here, we point. See Girl. We watch them look around, up, down, into the muddy waters, up at the moony skies. They see mud, mountain, smokestack, tree. River we hear them whisper. Moon. We tell them no. We say to these men the word, girl. Say Girl, we tell them. Say Girl until you see, till you hear, that Girl, G-I-R-L, and the sound that that word makes, when we say it, G-I-R-L—for us muddy brothers, it is a muddy river that rolls right off of our lips.

WHAT WE DO WITH THE FISH
AFTER WE GUT THE FISH

Peter Markus

We eat the fish.

Our mother fries up the fish in a cast iron skillet that spits up buttery fish fried grease every time she drops a bread crumb battered fish fillet into the pan. We sit at the kitchen table in front of our empty plates and listen to the pop and pizz and sizzle of the frying up fish. Just yesterday these fish were swimming in the muddy waters of our muddy river and now they are gutted and headless and chopped in half and about to be swallowed into our open mouths, our empty bellies. Our father is outside, in the shed, sharpening his knives. When all the fish have been fried up hard to a crisp shucked golden colored brown, our mother will tell us brothers to call in our father to come inside to eat the fish. Fish on, we will tell him. Come and get them while they're good and hot. Our father comes when we call. He tracks mud into our mother's kitchen. Our mother tells him look what you've done. He looks down at his boots and says the word mud. Our mother throws up her hands and then she throws the skillet of fried up fish at our father. The fish skid across the kitchen floor. Our father tells her that he and us sons caught and cleaned out the guts of those fish. Our mother tells our father he knows what he can do with those fish. Then she tells us how she hates fish and fish smells, how she hates this fishy river, how much she hates this fishy, smelly town. Leave, our father says to this. Our mother says maybe she will. They both turn and walk away, our father back outside, our mother into hers and our father's bedroom. Us brothers are left with the fish, are left to clean up the mess. We drop down onto our hands and knees onto the floor and begin to eat.

DIDDIM'S TRIALS

Roger Lathbury

Notwithstanding his admiration for Balzac, Tolstoy, Dreiser, and Oates, Ikke Diddim discovered, before he died, that he was a different kind of writer—a minimalist, in the tradition of Schwitters, Dadou, and the early Saroyan (Aram). Although the book he read most obsessively was Ellis' *Less Than Zero*, he had begun a novel, *Diddim's Trials*, which he planned to publish under a pseudonym, in the great European tradition:

On Friday 30 December in the year 19——, a well-to-do stock broker from Soho stepped confidently to the door of an obscure townhouse off Washington Square and rang the bell twice. His summons was not answered. He did not expect it to be.

Diddim intended to portray his repeated efforts—as writer, lover, communicator, and squatter—as a metaphor for the isolation and inhumanity of modern existence.

Then Diddim began editing. He erased the first sentence, paring the second two.

The summons, made twice, was not answered, as Diddim expected.

Better, he thought—terser, more mysterious, with a breathtaking lack of contextualization that dramatized the novel's central concerns. He folded the manuscript into shirt pocket size, hoping it would gestate, or de-gestate. He tried his former girlfriend, Sharon, who wasn't in, or wasn't answering her phone. Since the subletters of the flat where he slept returned in half an hour, he went outside to hustle his lunch, which he ate at 1 AM because the occupants slept nights.

The following evening was cold, dark, and moonless. Diddim shivered as he crossed McDougal. Luck was with him. He pulled the manuscript out of his pocket. Thanks to the size of the folded sheet, a single word stared up at him.

not

Laughing at how easily a novel could be completed, Diddim forgot where he was stepping: an open manhole.

Charon was ready.

READING GROUP DISCUSSION GUIDE

Denise Duhamel

1. Discuss the protagonist's "taboo purr" as she dips her forefinger into the "happy pink wax" pooling around the dripping candle. Why do you think she refers to the sticky paraffin as an "eerie halo?"

2. What vice is the protagonist's father trying to quell when he axes his ascots?

3. Why does the protagonist always associate the "slut" girl with pastoral images of blooming jutes and idyllic vales dotted with ewes?

4. What is the aim of the "idiot" boy who maims his gerbils? Why does the protagonist yawn instead of yelp?

5. What do the mother's reoccurring dreams of radon signify? Why does she continually say, "Get me another drink, darling," even when no one else is home?

6. Who, in your opinion, is the real goner? Is anybody actually resting in peace? (RIP, as the headstones say.)

7. We learn in chapter 4 that the protagonist's favorite letter is "Z." Notice all the zee sounds in the final paragraph of the novel—fizz, zipdrive, hazy buzzing. What is the significance of ending the book on the word "zero"?

SWEATERS

Nicholas DiChario

I fell in love with her beautiful sweaters. She wore a different one everyday. Solid ones, striped ones, loose ones, tight ones, bright ones, white ones. Cardigans, pullovers, short sleeves, long sleeves, crewnecks, v-necks, and daring cowls. She reminded me of Aunt Rita. When Aunt Rita died, our family donated over four hundred sweaters to the Salvation Army.

She worked at the newsstand, this girl, in a narrow slot behind a glass counter, on the ground floor of a corporate monolith. She was a dash of poly/cotton color in a blue/gray blur of corporate uniforms. "Been meaning to tell you," I said to her one morning. "Love your sweaters."

"Oh. Thank you."

"Thought you might like to go out sometime, you know, just the two of us—cup of coffee, dinner, film. You remind me of my Aunt Rita. She used to wear sweaters all the time, just like you. Such beautiful sweaters. Her favorite was a Scottish cashmere. We buried her in it."

While I stood waiting, she sold two lottery tickets, *The New York Times*, and a cup of coffee. The security guard popped in and told her that he'd finished his screenplay and was looking for an agent. Then we were alone. She leaned on the counter, scrunching the delicate chambray under her elbows, and said, "Did you ever wanna fuck your Aunt Rita?"

"God, no! Of course not! Are you joking? You're joking. Of course not!" I often spoke without thinking. Bad habit of mine.

"That's what I thought," said the girl.

She turned away to sell a pack of cigarettes, leaving behind a trace of static, and we never spoke again.

FROM THE TORRE LATINO

C.M. Mayo

There was this man who wanted to jump. He'd given his wallet to the elevator boy, his car keys to the janitor. He said, "*Estoy cansado.*" I'm tired, that's all he kept saying, I'm tired. He had hair the color of champagne, a double-breasted jacket, an alligator skin belt—and we wanted to help him, we really did. He kept taking in deep breaths, as if he were swallowing something enormous, and, as he held it over the ledge, shaking one ankle. A crowd gathered below, humming humming. Somewhere in the distance there was a siren, but it was going, not coming. The office manager leaned out on his elbows.

"Think of your children," he said, and things like that. The man said, "Please, I am so fucking tired."

And he tossed out his watch. It flashed like a small coin. And then it looked like what it was.

TO THE POET'S WIFE

J. David Stevens

You should not believe that poem about the plums. He didn't eat them so sweet and cold. I ate those plums, then wrote that note in his hand and laid two plum-pits bright as marbles on your table.

But he found that note and took those pits and ground them into powder, then wet that powder to make ink. Then took that note—that sorry excuse for a note—and crossed it through with plum-pit to make lines. Then gave it to you and said it was a poem.

I watched through your window, plum juice staining my chin. I had three more plums in my pocket for later.

But I also had hope, because here I saw a woman who knew the value of plums over poems and wouldn't take a man's word over the genuine article any day of the week. You failed me, my dear. You ate those syllables, making the plums in my belly less sweet. And then you kissed him, which probably kept him going for days.

I couldn't eat after that. I left the plums by your wall near the sprinkler. Later, my friend who pushes the wheelbarrow saw three new plum trees in your yard. "That fruit grew *fast*," he said. "Looks sweet."

But I was off plums by then. "You want a sure bet," I told him, "stick with oranges."

I did not tell him about the dreams I was having: plum trees as far as one could see. I did not tell him how words ruin desire— how poems make men want the thing itself but more than that thing, too.

In fact, I'm having trouble eating fruit at all. You have unmade me, dear. And for what? What did I do to you? Me, harmless, a simple eater of plums.

FINGERLINGS

Clint McCown

Eddie squinted into the yellow plastic tub beside him on the stoop. The fish were dead. He rubbed a stinging trickle of sweat from his eye and scooted deeper into the square of green shade beneath the fiberglass awning. Foolishly, he leaned back, scorching his sunburned shoulder on the trailer's aluminum wall.

"Goddamn shit!" he yelped, and sprang out into the yard. A chalky cloud of dust rose around his flip-flops.

His father leaned over the edge of the roof and pointed a tarladen brush down at him. "Boy, we don't use that kind of language." Then he turned back to his work, filling in the trailer's cracks and blisters.

Eddie looked away, toward the gravel patch where his brother Tom tinkered under the hood of their pickup.

But people did talk that way. Tom, Jeffy. Jim, who might go into the navy. Uncle Brick, who slept on their couch. Even his father, sometimes, late at night, with the music loud and his shirt off.

Jeffy stepped out onto the stoop and stretched, then wrinkled his nose at the yellow tub. "Christ, Eddie. These minnows are stinkin' up the whole damn yard."

"They ain't minnows," he said.

Jeffy looked more closely. "Okay, so they're fingerlings. Now go dump 'em someplace."

It was Tom's fault. When they'd come upon the school, so quick and silvery, stranded at the mouth of the culvert where the creek crossed under the road, Eddie had asked how many he should catch.

"Take all you can get, kiddo," Tom told him, laughing, and that's what he'd done, packing the mayonnaise jar full.

Too much life in too small a space.

Now he lifted up the tub and stared at the fingerlings through his own reflection on the fouled water. All their little faces looked the same.

MAN IN THE AUDIENCE

Jane McCafferty

The poet reading her work was not old yet, but her face was pained, her words were all for jax and blue chairs by windows or a bowl full of beets flung toward the sun. Nobody would eat the beets, but in a dog's dream they would change into hearts. (She had enough imagination to turn broken glass into a river, a bleeding fist into a cloud.) But no human loves appeared in those poems.

A man in the audience, also a poet, a man who had distrusted the world ever since his father had nearly killed him that night when he was nine, we had never seen him listen so hard the way he listened to the visiting poet. Gradually shards of his face fell on the floor and revealed this new face.

This new face bore only a family resemblance to the old face. The new face was soft with light that had landed there like radiance that had long been homeless. Pure tenderness, a hint of a reverent smile as his chin lowered down, even in a deepening shyness. How naked he looked in the face of her loneliness! He was a new child in her arms, rocked by cold lullabies.

And then she put him down; the reading was over, the words were gone. He walked home alone in his coat, chin lifted, lips tight as ever, as if nothing at all had happened.

FREEZER JESUS

Antonio Vallone

"Captain ah the shrimpin' boats ain't called in months." Curtis Wood McNeese spoke deliberately into the cassette recorder's tiny microphone slots. "No odd jobs. Unemployment's nearly runned out. Can't make swine out ah water, ya know."

Curtis squinted one milky blue eye and leaned back in his chair. The reporter nodded.

"Three cardinals, red as boiled mudbugs, landed on top ah my freezer." Curtis cocked his head in its direction.

The reporter swung his feet off the trailer's porch railing and stood up. He took a notebook out of his sportcoat pocket and started jotting notes.

"I'll be damned if the freezer's tune didn't change somehow. Started hummin' like a band ah angels. Rays ah sunlight broke through the clouds. The freezer lit up like the Fourth of July." Curtis dabbed at his eyes with his bathrobe's sleeve. "I saw the image ah Jesus on the door, smiling, reaching out like he was givin' me something."

The reporter walked over to the freezer, looking it over like a used Studebaker. He spread out the palm of his right hand and placed it against the door. He shut his eyes and held his hand still for a few seconds. Then he opened the door and shuffled through the packages: fish sticks, loaves of bread dough.

"Of course not everyone could see Him," Curtis's voice rose like a tent evangelist's, booming. "But I knew He wanted me to spread the word. And word ah Him did get around. I told my neighbors and relations. They told theirs. Local paper sent a reporter. TV station from Lake Charles sent a crew out. Put the town ah Sulphur on the map for somethin' more than its stink."

The reporter arched an eyebrow and took a whiff of the air.

"Once the story went out on the wire services, people started comin' from miles around. God bless 'em, they pulled they's cars and trucks onto my lawn, parkin' in rows like they was at a drive-in movie. The double feature was salvation and healin'." Curtis paused. "But my lawn was gettin' ruined."

The reporter shut the cover of his notebook and slipped it back into his pocket.

"I had to do somethin', being out ah work an' all. So I started passing empty lard buckets around. For lawn maintenance, ya know."

The reporter looked out at the narrow strip of hard-packed dirt and gravel beyond the trailer's porch, blades of grass poking up in sparse patches.

"The buckets came back filled. I could barely lift 'em." Curtis smiled and rested his folded hands on his stomach. "Like water into wine. It was a miracle, I tell ya. There ain't no other way to describe it."

THE SECRET LIFE OF WOMEN

Alyce Miller

Melinda knew the girl's name and what she looked like. She also knew how the girl dressed and walked, and which apartment was hers. She even knew her phone number, which had the numerals 2 and 0, just like the girl's age, repeated twice in succession. She knew the girl's major, and what time she took the History of the Harlem Renaissance. Melinda knew this, because her husband Edward Beaucaire taught the course.

Now before you go thinking that Melinda was a jealous woman, always looking under the bed, let it be made clear that no, she wasn't and no, she didn't. In fact, Melinda was about the most un-jealous woman we'd ever known. But she wasn't a pushover. Fine as Edward was, and we mean *fine*, Melinda wasn't one to think she was lucky just to have a BMW (black man working) and so overlooked the nonsense. For one thing, Melinda had too much on the ball herself. She might have loved Edward (we knew how much she did), but our girl was not about to let any man make a fool of her.

So you can forget about some jealous confrontation (of the *leave my man alone or I'll whup your ass* variety). Or any of those crazy stories about throwing pots of hot grits or snatching someone's hairpiece off her head. I know you're wondering what Melinda did do. We speculated. Time passed. We held our breath, murmured among ourselves. Edward Beaucaire won an award and Melinda threw a big barbecue in their backyard to celebrate. There was a band. And do you know that girl had the nerve to show up? Well, Melinda got up to sing—she had a beautiful voice—she looked right at the girl and when she hit her high note, that girl burst into flames. And then she looked right over at us, but we were scattering like birds.

THE EXPATRIATE

Alyce Miller

"The world's sure changed since I was a girl." Cilla's mother spread the newspaper out on the kitchen table. "Listen to this…"

Cilla at the stove stared with disgust at the fried egg swimming in oil, a fat yellow eye in a pan, eerie and nerve-wracking. She herself wouldn't eat eggs.

"You know that psycho-killer?" said her mother. "Says here he actually *gutted* them while they struggled. Can you imagine? Just the sheer physical strength it would take?"

Cilla flipped the egg, inadvertently breaking the top membrane. Yellow goo oozed into the oil and hardened in jagged lines along the edge of the pan like detaching arteries. Annoyed, she yanked up the pan and dumped the mutilated egg into her mother's trash.

"Says here he strung them upside down first. The only thing I ever gutted was fish," muttered her mother. "That was back when your father used to bring them home. Guess I gutted dead chickens too."

"I'm going to start over," Cilla said, cracking a new egg into the pan.

When it fell in perfect symmetry into the sizzling oil, she experienced a small, unexpected flash of disappointment.

Her mother misunderstood.

"I already said you can stay with me as long as you need, no one's rushing you to make up your mind. Dear Abby says lots of grown children… "

Cilla cracked a second egg. It dropped elegantly beside the other into the sizzling oil. "I meant the eggs."

"Cook those good now." Her mother reached for the coffee. "D'you know a foreign woman from my church eats her eggs raw? She'll get salmonella."

"Not all eggs have salmonella," said Cilla.

"Well, it's not normal eating raw eggs."

The edges of the eggs curled up and blackened. The yokes bubbled. Cilla didn't answer, just turned the flame higher.

THE SEASONS

Alyce Miller

A long time ago I had a different husband. In winter I kept him stashed in a small closet next to the front bedroom. He rarely took food, but he was clean and neat, and made almost no noise. Nights I couldn't sleep we talked by tapping Morse code on the shared wall. On warm spring days I would unpack him and carry him out to the convertible and prop him up on the front seat like a little suitcase. We would drive back roads for hours in silence. He could be moody and unpredictable, so I never pressed him for details, nor did I seek his opinions on matters of importance. I intuited all his needs. Out back was a little doghouse where he liked to sleep. Sometimes, in summer, he'd stay chained in the yard all afternoon, eying the carpenter bees. He never howled, or at least neighbors never reported that he did. He would wait for me to return. If the evenings were hot, I'd take ice water out for us to share and he'd lap his gratefully with his small round tongue. Then we'd sit and listen to the cicadas shimmer in the trees. Last week, when he was curling up in my lap, I noticed the briefest shadow fall across his unshaven cheek. The silver maple was dropping its hand-shaped leaves into the grass. "Dog," I said to my husband, "it's about time to pack you away again." He turned mournful eyes to me, offered one small whimper. I think he also muttered, "seasons are irrelevant," but he was wrong. All change is treachery. By the time the snow fell, he had found a new wife.

THE RIVER INSIDE HER

Paola Corso

There once was a river inside her so she swam. She swam and swam and floated by a tender rock where boys counted hobos on freight trains, by a family pitching horseshoes at a cornroast, drifting, drifting by a woman sealing a jar of jam with wax. She drifted farther still to a box of checkers under a Christmas tree until she could drift no more, so she paddled.

She paddled and paddled and kicked beyond a blue island where she remembered the day a pilot and her plane disappeared and a hero's baby was kidnapped until she could kick no more, so she thrashed.

She thrashed and thrashed and bobbed for air in a rapid current where she grabbed onto tree branches and shiny possessions with plugs whose long electrical cords reeled her in to the riverbank until she could bob no more, so she lay there.

She lay there and lay there and basked in a sun so strong it evaporated the river inside her, until she could bask no more, so she prayed.

She prayed and prayed and reflected on her last breath of life before they wheeled in a machine with three images to resuscitate her.

When they pulled the lever, a lemon, a banana, and a cherry appeared, but she did not open her eyes. When they pulled the lever again, two lemons and a cherry appeared, but she did not open her eyes.

When they pulled the lever once more, three lemons appeared and she awoke, inhaling and exhaling long enough to touch the tender rock protruding from her bosom then to roll over, leaving a puddle left from the river inside her until it too evaporated down to a drop too small for even the wind to swallow.

HARMON'S DILEMMA

Corey Mesler

Harmon wrote his wife a letter outlining the various reasons he had been unfaithful to her. He folded the paper neatly and placed it inside an envelope and put it next to the mixmaster where she was sure to find it.

Harmon then went for a long drive. He needed to clear his head and, somehow, alleviate the guilt that was building in him like a heart attack. It was barely dawn; there was still a little silver sliver of moon above the refinery. Harmon looked around at the town where he and his family had made their refuge. It all seemed meet and right to him. Harmon was sorry he had cheated on his wife. He was sorry he wrote that letter.

By the time Harmon had turned around and gotten himself back into his home his wife and children were lined up in the living room with money in their hands. They were buying off Harmon's share in the family and cutting him loose.

The first thing Harmon did in the motel room where he landed was to dial his lover's number. The phone rang and rang. But she was far away now—how could Harmon know this?—meeting a man who had been married to the same woman for 27 years. Harmon listened to that dead ringing for a full minute. His life was shrinking fast and he didn't have the first clue how to slow things down.

THE PSYCHIC TAKES A GREYHOUND

Susan Hubbard

A woman wearing a headscarf strewn with shamrocks says she's leaving the bus at Vegas. She says she's feeling lucky.

The psychic looks into her eyes and sees playing cards fanned across a green table. The cards blur, turn into tombstones.

"When's the last time you saw your doctor?" the psychic says.

"Last month," the woman says. "He told me—"

"Never mind," the psychic says. She knows the woman has cancer and won't last past Easter.

"Make peace with your daughter," the psychic says. "And call her soon, before the end of March."

The woman nods, slowly.

The psychic says, "Good luck to you."

A young man boards the bus at Vegas and ignores the empty seats to sit next to the psychic. His eyes are bloodshot, and his t-shirt smells of whiskey and a woman's tears. The psychic sees him behind bars, but not for another year.

When he stands up at Salt Lake City, she says to him, "Stay away from the redhead. Take my advice. Or it means five years out of your life."

The man swears at the psychic and leaves the bus.

His seat is taken almost at once by a man who moves from across the aisle.

"How do you know these things?" he asks.

His left eye is gray and full of money. His right eye is blue and full of love. The psychic pats her fluffy hair and takes her glasses off.

"It's just a game I play," she says. "But tell me about yourself. Tell me everything."

And she knows they'll be together, until he tells her the first lie.

UNDER GLASS

Susan Hubbard

He had a reputation as a womanizer, a lady's man. But he told her he was simply a man who appreciated women. When she asked, he said he really couldn't remember how many women he'd loved. She could only wonder—was it sixty? Six hundred? A thousand?

Women seemed to have entered and quit his life without rancor, leaving only gifts. The shelves in his apartment were a clutter of love-tokens: heart-shaped paperweights and etchings of nudes, brass statues of cats, wooden cufflink boxes, inkwells and Venetian glass pens. She looked at the objects, but never touched them. She tried to imagine the hands of the women who had bestowed them.

She wondered which ones sent him birthday cards and which ones telephoned him after midnight. In bed it was the same—she wondered who had taught him this caress that whispered flattery. When she asked, he said, "I don't recall their names."

One summer afternoon they sat in a restaurant at a window table. He wore sunglasses against the glare.

"I love *you*," he said, "and no one else."

She clasped her hands and looked at him across the table. Reflected in the lenses of his sunglasses was the image of a woman passing by outside.

"Marry me," he said. The image of the woman froze.

"I know why you want me to marry you," she said. "You're running out of shelf space."

The woman hit the window with her hand, and he looked up. The woman smiled and waved.

"Wow," he said. "It's Michelle."

NERVES

David Booth

On opening day a girl much too young to be smoking tossed her half-smoked cigarette into a trashcan and entered the building. Once inside, she took the elevator to the top floor, where everybody was waiting. When the elevator doors finally opened, she went straight for the stairwell and, running back down to where she came from, found both the trashcan ablaze and the crowd she had always imagined.

BACK

Sherrie Flick

After the storm, my clock started running backwards. I told this to my boyfriend, Bob, when he called from Toronto. He said, "Impossible."

He explained the motor, how it wasn't designed to reverse; how it couldn't possibly rotate in the opposite direction. I was doing dishes while he talked, the receiver jammed in between my ear and shoulder, the cord bouncing in and out of the suds.

"Must be something else," he said, then he said, "Impossible," again as if the discussion was over. I knew he was impatient to talk about other things like Nietzsche and baseball.

I watched minutes ticking back from where they had come. Soon it was five minutes before Bob had called. I let the drain out of the sink; I dried my hands on the kitchen towel. I hung up the phone in the middle of a sentence about R.B.I.s, smiling to myself.

I knew if I waited long enough I simply wouldn't know Bob anymore. The thought turned and turned, then settled snugly in my head. I put some water in the kettle, turned the flame on high, and sat down at my kitchen table.

The phone was ringing and my instinct was to pick it up and apologize. But now, time was flying back and back and it seemed my life would just go on forever and ever—except in the other direction.

Soon I wouldn't be saying hi to Bob in philosophy class. Instead I would sit on the other side of the room and meet Steve, a kinder man with an interest in houseplants and the capacity to believe in the impossible.

THE CHEERLEADER

Liz Mandrell

"I want you to call me Laura from now on." Laura cracked six eggs in a bowl, beat them swiftly and poured them into the hot skillet.

"I want to still call you Mom." Chrisanne kicked off her white K-Swiss tennis shoes and picked up a handful of mismatched socks from the laundry basket at her feet. Her Sacred Heart pom-pons, crumbled in a heap, lay next to her book bag and lunchbox on top of the piano.

"I prefer Laura."

"What's wrong with Mom? You're still my mother." Chrisanne laid the socks in a row on the counter like suspects in a line-up, looking for a match.

"I will always be your mom. I just don't want that name any more."

"Is this some sort of mid-life crisis?"

The front door slammed *whack!* Footsteps jarred up the hardwood stairs two at a time.

A door slam, another thud, then silence.

"The freak is home."

"Don't call your brother that." Laura chopped onions and peppers and tomatoes on the cutting board, then into the eggs. "He's having a hard time with the divorce."

"He's a freak."

Laura banged the spatula on the skillet.

"Laura sounds like a cheerleader's name," Chrisanne said and started coupling socks without looking—booties with anklets, crew socks with knee highs.

Laura slipped the omelet out of the skillet onto a waiting plate. She poured herself a glass of wine and leaned against the counter to look at her daughter. Silence filled the room like a held breath.

"I was a cheerleader," Laura said. "A long time ago."

Chrisanne glared at her mother and with one arm, a backhand swat from a forward vault mount, swept all the socks back into the basket.

WHAT THE WEDDING PHOTOS SAY

Nickole Brown

1. She is beautiful. She is nervous and pale but beautiful in white brought all the way from Venice just for her. Just as planned, she has on a bright enough shade of lipstick to hide the downward turn of the corners of her mouth. With a red this bright, it looks like more of a pout than a frown.

2. He is drinking. At least a shot or two before the ceremony. You can tell from the red tips of his ears. He has realized that the groom in a wedding is little better than a prop

3. Her mama is a radiant and angry diva in a low cut silver dress. She has smashed out almost two packs worth of cigarettes one by one with the toe of her tiny silver heel

4. His mother is radiant and angry. She can barely smile for the camera and she has bunched the long lacey sleeves up past her elbows to show how hard she is working. Seven dozen gardenias have come in wilted and brown.

5. Her stepfather is trying. He has never worn a tux before, and he looks as awkward as Lita did dabbing her mouth with a linen napkin. He holds his shoulders back too much, exposing his large, crooked cummerbund.

6. His father is trying. He is shaking hands with people he normally wouldn't even talk to, and the last bit of his son's whisky has turned his ears red too.

7. The bridesmaids are uncomfortable in their matching periwinkle gowns. Jenna dances at the reception barefoot, and the other girls have hiked the sides of their dresses up to their underwear, the backs unzipped and dangling.

8. The groomsmen are hung over. They eat all of the tortilla pinwheels before the guests even get in line. Justin changes into a kilt at the reception and dances with girls barely out of high school.

9. Her grandmother is not there. She is in Florida staring into a photo of her own wedding day. She breaks every one of her porcelain windowsill birds. Later she blames it on the skateboarders and calls the condo manager to show him what they've done.

ISN'T IT RELI(E)VING?

Davis Schneiderman

International Fex, corporate leader, routinely suspects that his underlings act so vain and petty because they can't help but fawn over his stunning good looks—becoming mere reflections of himself when in his presence. Still, something in Fex's life isn't quite right; he has been unable to enjoy his mansions and pools and endless cadres of beautiful women in the easygoing manner in which many of his fawning friends enjoy their lesser models. Fex calls his shrink for a midnight consultation and by 2 a.m. they discover that Fex is afraid of intimacy so he should try to date a different kind of woman from his cyborg of the week because he is getting old so quick and his back already crinks and shudder under the weight of encroaching death and/or dismemberment at the annual stockholder meeting.

Accordingly, Fex has to announce that fourth quarter profits will be off the stated goal by an unsettling 2%, which causes his group of corpulent investors—many of whom are long term friends and potential supporters of his future political action campaigns and exploratory committees—to point their heads directly at the ground as he descends from the podium. Rather than scrutinizing some lower element of his Italian ensemble, they instead stare into the twists of the polished floor, no doubt intent on their personal reflections.

"This can't be good for me," says Fex to no one in particular, and when he enters the men's room to relieve himself, two of his long-time associates clam up just as his face emerges in the steamy mirror.

"This isn't happening. I'm not here," says Fex under his breath to no one in particular. Not even to himself. Staring closely at his yellow reflection while pissing, he disappears once again into the stream of everyone else.

WHEN THE MEN CAME HOME

Sean Thomas Dougherty

When the men came home from work you could hear a crow caw in their clothes. They were covered in ash and soot, covered in grease and Coke dust, covered head to foot, they washed until their hands came clean. Uncle Louis always opened a beer, a Pabst Blue Ribbon with a pretty blue label he'd peel for me, and Uncle Ike would come over too for Grandma's cooking and would swing me into the air and they'd all hold me up "like something to see." Lena once scolded me and pulled my ears pretending to be jealous—but in some way all the men were always looking at her, as if they knew who held their History in their hands.

The house would be filled with a loud laughter and even when they come home drinking first there was never trouble that I can recall. There was only potatoes boiling that I helped Grandma peel, and carrot rinds on the floor, and a bubbling stew, or meat cooked in a big roasting pan, like in just before the big snows came when the duck blinds dotted the frozen lake and Ike came in with handle of webbed feet in his fist: Green-headed mallards dangling from a wrapped wire—that night our faces ran with thick juices and I saw mama nearly weep as she leaned into my father, and I could feel myself falling asleep in her lap that night, and the moon was like *a present in the sky*, she said this, *all wrapped in white like it means something more than far away*. Her all wrapped in warm, her arms, and the aftertimes, the openings and hurts they held. That house rocked hard toward whatever held for us. All of us big with laughter and longing, even then so small I could fit inside the sewing, and Lena and Aunt Bettie and my mother knitting socks by the fire: at their feet a basket of yarn unspooling.

EULOGY (FOR MY FATHER)

Susannah Breslin

In the weeks after my father's death, I found in my head a terrible pounding. I put my fingers to my temples, but the world around me reverberated with its throbbing. Inside of my head, I went to see a doctor. From the waiting room, I was led into an examining room, where I lay down on a couch. "How are you feeling?" the doctor said. I looked up to the blue ceiling above me, and I saw it was covered with the glowing stars and planets of my childhood bedroom. What could I say? "You have dreams," said the doctor. "Tell me one." I began. "I am riding on a train to New York City. One of the other passengers is my father. I move through the train car, slowly circling him. I realize my father didn't die, he's been alive all along. But I cannot speak to him." The doctor sat silent. Then, he delivered his diagnosis. "You are mentally pregnant," he declared. "Not with a potential life, but with a person, indeed, a whole life. Your father lives on in you. But to hear him depends upon your ability to tell the difference between him and yourself." He told me, "An operation is necessary." With his pencil, the doctor opened up my head. Suddenly, my father was again before me. I saw his hands, his face, his body. Then, he was gone, out and through the window of the doctor's office. From the window, I stood watching my father roll in the wet green grass under his apple tree. I called to my father, "Father, how will I fill all the empty time stretching out before me?" My father, now fallen, told me, "Who can tell? I have made a place." And with that, a dark wind blew my father away. I was left behind, alone. But, inside the room, the universe was burning around me.

THE STEEPLEJACK

Jesse Lee Kercheval

The steeplejack, Tadeus Szyhalski, is singing, paint brush in hand, standing astride the globe that is the water tower of B——, Wisconsin, pop. 603. He is up so high even the soles of his boots are above the town's two church towers, one Catholic, one Lutheran, in a countryside of towns with two churches, one Catholic, one Lutheran. In the soles of his feet, he feels the town wake, water hums from the tank on its way to fill toilets, coffee pots, to wash last night's dishes, lovers sticky with sex. Below him, the town swimming pool begins to fill. In Poland, he painted the pitched roofs of cathedrals, in Florida he painted a water tower to look like an orange. This job is simple, silver paint, then a big red "B".

The high school band, dressed like Hussars, are marching on the edge of town. In the distance, one of their soldiers is drumming. Tadeus Szyhalski sees her tri-cornered hat, her pigtail tied with a bow. He has a daughter, grown, who lives in Warsaw, but she was never musical.

The next thing he sees is a flock of crows, in a still further field, who, having discovered the scarecrow's not real, settle as one to peck his straw head, to knock off his hat which is blown by a wind from the west where clouds have begun to gather over the distant Mississippi.

In the late afternoon, at last, the echoing tower falls silent with the town—taps shut, all clothes at last washed and hung out to dry. Tadeus Szyhalski finishes the "B", careful not to let the paint drip. The last thing Tadeus sees from his scaffold is the tornado as it drops from the clouds like the dark finger of God and heads, spinning, toward the town.

AFTER THE FUNERAL, JOE TELLS A STORY

Jesse Lee Kercheval

One night, long ago, Joe said, he'd been south with a partner when the moon came up with a ring around it like a lasso. It shone so bright, the cactus started blooming. Then they heard music. So high up, it made your ears itch. Made his donkey crazy. She took off, they followed, and found her leaning against a giant saguaro, watching a woman nurse a baby. Sitting balanced on the arms of the cactus were two men wearing robes whiter than any Chinaman could bleach them. Each man had three pairs of wings, one pair to cover his feet, one to cover his eyes, and another pair to fly with. Then the baby sat up. His eyes focusing on each in turn. Like an augur bit, Joe said, cut clean to the core, testing what minerals you were made of. He and his partner left the baby all the gold they'd found. Even their beans, their coffee. Later another prospector caught up with them. Watch your ass, he said. Bandits killed a woman and her baby. Just for their supplies.

And that, said Joe, is why we all got to suffer a little while longer.

THE BELT OF RULE

Laurence Davies

"Here," says Sheila, "Wear my father's belt. Genuine oxblood leather."

Rudy the lecher puts it on, buckling at the third hole out. "What do you think?"

"Makes you look like him. Slender. Responsible."

But father-in-law had worn it tighter. Rudy sees the crease beside the inmost hole.

That night, while Sheila's marshalling her pens and mopping up her desk, Rudy slips out for a Cuba libre. At the High Hat Bar a woman looks his way, tapping one heel against her barstool, licking pillowy lips. The moment he licks back, an ache throttles his belly. He's eaten nothing bloating (no beans, no wholemeal bread, no undercooked potatoes), but the belt has tightened on him cruelly. He has to let it out but no, not now, not with those pulsing lips so close. Yet if he doesn't let it out, sure as a power saw the belt will slice him through the midriff. Closing his eyes, he thinks of mountain spruce and icy streams. Far away he hears the clack of disappointed heels.

It happens again at an office party, the moment a fingernail (he guesses whose, he knows it's purple) infiltrates his jacket. It happens on Union Square as he gapes at violet eyes and standing nipples. He feels his guts mash, his waist blister underneath the penitential cinch.

He buys another belt, cocoa-brown, innocuous, and sneaks a trial glance or two. Now he can gaze or even wink without a pang. The brown belt simply lets him be.

"Where is Pa's belt?" asks Sheila. "You haven't worn it once this week, not even once. What's wrong with you?"

"I got too big."

"Wear his necktie then, black and blue, the old school colors. You'll never wriggle out of that."

HUGH OF PROVO

Tom Bradley

> ...*O deere child, I halsen thee,*
> *in vertu of the hooly Trinitee,*
> *Tel me what is thy cause for to synge,*
> *Sith that thy throte is kut to my semynge?*
> -Prioress' Tale, 645-8

A disturbed adolescent, the daughter of inbred survivalist neighbors, creepy-crawls our backyard with her cat. She steals our few grape wads and leaves spoor among the unmown pear mush: Marie Osmond-brand perfume atomizers, toy Tampax tubes.

Even allowing for accelerated maturation rates among rural polygamist females, I estimate she's too old for toys. Every night, all night, her ashen cat copulates with everything furred the neighborhood has to offer, under our bagged air conditioner, though my wife sleeps clear through.

Sometimes these two marauders seep through the drapes in vaporous form and reintegrate on the skin of my chest, where the larger, more anthropomorphic one squats in a vulgar position, something furred, taloned, coiling around her plump limbs.

She hisses in my ear:

Medieval times are coming to your neighborhood, Tom. Your Catholic spouse, who accepts spirits and so can dismiss them, will snore through it all. But you, you aging acidhead, with your hoed rows of secular humanist psilocybin cubensis, you're in for it.

Walpurgisnacht will erupt in the dark, not mushrooms.

We will turn into a sweet-singing boy, and you into a Jew. The fiberglass of your greenhouse will melt down into a cesspool, and we'll see who seduces whom.

ERATO: THE POET AT SIXTY

William Heyen

I

I hadn't seen her in about twenty years. She'd been an enigmatic presence in my American Literature I class—From the Puritans to the Romantics—then had dropped out when she couldn't keep up her course journal of responses to readings. Then she'd enrolled in & dropped out of my American Transcendentalist Writers.

When she stood in front of me, last in line, after my bookstore poetry reading, I didn't at first recognize her, but then saw the reddish-brown jewel—maybe a garnet—embedded in her nostril. Her ponytailed blonde hair had become a red buzzcut, she now seemed anorexic but, yes, it was her, that harried, even cornered look still playing in her eyes.

Our chat squirmed. She had an old book of mine with her & asked me to write something poetic in it. I inscribed it in memory of her years at our school, & added two lines from Christina Rossetti: "And if thou wilt, remember,/And if thou wilt, forget." When she read my inscription, she grimaced a smile. I saw a diamond embedded in an incisor. When she noticed that I noticed it, she laughed, then ran the tip of her tongue over it.

Something else was going on, something, another color. Then I realized that she'd pierced her tongue. What seemed to be a pearl rode the pink & gray oyster meat. She held her mouth open & extended her tongue so that I could see it....

II

I still had her journal in my desk. Staccato, what there was of it.
Some entries written in gem-like sheared-off unintelligible musical
phrases reminiscent of Paul Celan. Write poetry, I'd responded in
a margin, but not for this course. In her last entry, she'd dwelled
on a teacher, maybe me, & quoted Walt Whitman as she thought
of parting the shirt from her teacher's bosom-bone, plunging her
tongue to his bare-stript heart, reaching till she felt his beard,
reaching till she held his feet. Then, blank pages.

A garnet & a diamond & a pearl, & where else, I wondered,
before I laid her down for good.

EXPERIENCE

William Heyen

During my junior year in college I lived above a garage two blocks from campus. I had to cross railroad tracks to get to my classes ... & I had to get to this particular class this particular morning, my professor had warned, or I'd be out of luck—I'd cut six or eight times already. I was weaker than a dullard in those days. The only bit of information that stuck in my mind from this course in the ancient writers was that a seagull had mistaken old Aeschuylus's bald head for a rock & had dropped a clam onto it—class dismissed.

Winter, heavy snow falling. I was running as best I could, hungover, huffing my bad breath. The eight o'clock bells were tolling from Hartwell Hall's tower. Maybe, because of the snow, class would begin a few minutes late & I'd be okay.

But a train was coming. I could hear its slow rumble, its intermittent steam whistle as it approached the crossing I was lurching toward. My problem was that these trains were long, sometimes ten minutes long, freightcar after freightcar, hundreds of freightcars clacking west to Buffalo. I had to get across the tracks before the train cost me my basketball eligibility.

I was almost there. To my left, maybe a hundred feet away, the train appeared, blurred black in the snow. I lumbered, the train got closer, my legs were lead & my footing uncertain. I reached the crossing, did not hesitate, dove across maybe thirty feet in front of the cow-catcher, sprawled on the sidewalk face first, my textbook embedding itself in a snowbank the way the clam must have embedded itself in Aeschuylus's skull. I was hurting—bruised ribs, a sprained knee that made me miss two games. For a few seconds before managing to grunt myself to my feet, I sat in the snow & looked back at that satanic engine. The train was already past. This time, there were no freightcars, only the lone locomotive plowing its track.

COLD TRUTH, BRIGHT AS A COIN

Christine Boyka Kluge

She coughs the hidden gold coin into his waiting palm. It is her last. He wipes it off on the corner of his wool cape, holds it up to the gaze of the winter sun. The sunlight is the color of pale ale. He has spent his own light elsewhere. On the face of the coin, the profile of a woman wearing a crown looks away. He bites the coin to test its truth. Early March, winter's end. Cold truth, bright as a coin.

The long season has left them with only a few smoked fish. They hang on a line between trees like dull charms on a necklace. The man and the woman share the dark rooms, nothing more. Perhaps a thin blanket of watery blue. The house sits by the edge of the tarnished river. In the mornings, she breaks the ice with her heel to dip her tin cup. A frail spiral of smoke drifts toward the sun like a smudged word.

The boom and crack of loosened river ice startles them from their separate thoughts. When the coin drops from his unfeeling fingers, it rolls into the thawing river at the end of the path. He watches a seam in the water tear open to silver. For a moment, the silver fractures into flecks of platinum and bronze, dancing like tossed change, like idle wishes. She searches his blank white face, his chapped fists. The snow is melting, dropping from branches, shrinking into bright nooses around the black rocks.

THE KILLER CLOWNS

Barry Silesky

A string breaks, clay & violet splat dirt all over the kitchen. Who wouldn't laugh? Fat dot dresses, red bulb noses, those clowns are a riot. Look at the colors, the glowing tent that draws us to them is irresistible. When the babies stagger down the hall in dad's shoes, Mom howls. They want a hat to wear. The tv preacher's caught with a teenager. The President's nominee chases women, likes his wine. We all giggle at them stumbling through town with those silly guns, but we know those clowns are dangerous. When they fire, the beam wrapping the innocent drunk in a cotton candy cocoon is almost beautiful. Time to put the kids to bed. Have another beer & I'll make some popcorn. At least we'll have peace to enjoy the rest of the movie. Ron's no fool; he doesn't need another kid to know what they mean. His wife hopes he'll forget the condom, but at least there's some money this way, all night to play & plenty of sleep. Ours wake so early, we're glad when the company leaves. It's when they open their mouths that our laugh catches. A growl from somewhere we can't see, then those teeth we do, and someone else is gone. What could they want? If only we knew, we might figure a way to make room, get out of the way, stop them. One walks along the rows of cocoons they've made from everyone who found them, dips a glass straw into the pink and sucks, stumbles off drunk on the potion. They grow from popcorn they spread, more every minute. This evil's so ridiculous we can't stop laughing. Sinhalese massacred in Sri Lanka, hundreds dead in Venezuelan riots—so far away it reminds us of our luck. If we pay attention, we can stop those babies before they dump their food all over the floor, tear up the mail, climb to pull down another glass. Every day they're faster. The crack dealing killer found guilty is out on parole too soon, but with luck it won't be our neighborhood. They can do anything, they're eating the world, they're grinning, they're taking off. Then the hero shoots off a nose, the thing disappears and the whole room's hysterical. The townspeople go for their guns. It's pure relief to know the clowns will be stopped.

The MAMMOTH Book of Miniscule Fiction

HERMIT CRAB

Stephen Gibson

It was a hermit crab, a boy gift, masculine, something only a male would give, one to another, as a birthday present. It smelled of ocean, hidden depths, uncharted bottoms, muck, mysteries in darkness. In its segmented armor, five probing legs and one enormous pincer, it carried a spiraled, hard-shelled world on its back in a plastic container, abandoning one shell world for another whenever it suited.

So he bought it, stopped at the pet store next to the supermarket where he went in to pick up a cake—after his wife, his ex-, always a day late and a dollar short, called him that morning, asked whether he'd forgotten what day it was and whether he cared, asked why she even bothered.

So he dressed, hurried, rang the doorbell—white cake-box held by its string, clear plastic container, packet of crab food taped to its handle. His boy answered—horrified, ran to his mother, screamed that his daddy had brought him a spider. His wife, seeing it, shouted he was crazy, he had to be crazy, as she pulled the boy into the juncture between her legs. He was crazy. Pushed the plastic container away from them. Pushed him through the hallway to the door. He had to be crazy to buy something like that for his son. It's a hermit crab, he hollered, raising the white cake-box and the plastic container like two lanterns—her fists raining against him in the hallway. A hermit crab, he shouted. But powerless. Her tangle of arms and legs moving against him, forcing him backward.

GOATBOY CONSIDERS WINTER

Natalia Rachel Singer

Goatboy comes to Mrs. Cups to take the waters. Up in her loft she suckles him, and then she writes a poem. This is their arrangement.

Goatboy is twenty-six, Mrs. Cups forty-two. They met at a psychic convention in Seattle, each presiding at competing Tarot tables, his crowded with hungry women. On his break, he sauntered over and asked for a reading. It was all there: the two gold goblets, the young boy in tights slinging wands, and herself, The Queen of Cups, posing languidly in her garden, with cleavage.

Since that day they've had their scenes, but mostly they work it through. He adores her completely, when he's in town. Sometimes his girlfriends leave messages on her answering machine: "Tell him to bring ham"; "Lambskins, with Anita Baker tapes"; "Maywine." She's the Poet Laureate of Vashon Island and got a grant to do a series: "Goatboy Cooks with Olive Oil," "Goatboy Climbs the Space Needle." Without him she'd be obliged to write about the patriarchy, or her cats.

When Goatboy arrives in the only blizzard in centuries, his Jeep stalls on the floating bridge. Thumbing, he gets picked up by a busload of teens on an outing to study snow. "Stay with us to build caves," the kids insist. The driver's a feline redhead from Walla Walla and he's tempted. "Sing," she commands, but when he picks up his guitar all that comes out are tributes to Mrs. Cups—those pimento red lips, briny and alert, those angel food cake breasts. He borrows a boy's snowshoes and plows his way over, his ardent tracks a zipper through the hemlock.

SULTAN

Natalia Rachel Singer

Ruby says she was once a sultan's wife in Persia. The sultan whipped his camels but had a gentle streak only she inspired. He sang sad songs of war while she baked almond cakes for his journeys. When he returned, she dabbed pomegranate on her lips, rubbed bee-balm on his skin, anointed him like holy parchment. At night she wore a gown of sheer gauze like a giant bandage. She doesn't remember the wounds.

In this life she is chunky, does Deal-A-Meal every June. Her husband was a cheater but she sort of got away. As her best friend, I help all I can. So I took her to Orlando, but all she could say was how the white sands in Persia smelled like honeysuckle. At the mall she paused at every bench to stare at babies. She kneeled before the mirror when we were trying on power blazers and demonstrated how to bow. *I bore princes once*, she whispered. *Twelve children, all boys.* She calculated the ages her children would be if this life's sultan hadn't made her abort. I had to pin her to the makeover counter to stop her from phoning him to ask why.

Oh Ruby. In Florida we got high on the manatees, the key lime pie, on those astronauts who gave us this planet in 3-D. But after we'd screamed our heads off on the *Back to the Future* ride she confessed she was still really stuck. I listed his girlfriends, like hurricanes, but she wasn't hearing me. *Think*, I said. *Think about what you're doing!* She said, *I could ask you the same, you big bully!* She paid a psychic in Casa Dega to channel messages from the sultan. I rode along for the view.

ONE THING YOU MUST NEVER DO

Angus Woodward

She might look young if you come in and find her smoking little brown fragrant things. When you ask if they're clove cigarettes, you'll find her laugh half chilling and half inviting. Ignore her. Just go about your business, go out and prune the bushes you were hired to prune, paint the shed you were hired to paint. Otherwise you'll draw closer to get a better sniff and she'll tell you they're ginger cigarettes she made herself. Next thing you know you'll be in the kitchen straining to hear her shouted instructions, looking for the ginger and the *phyllo* dough, getting sleepy and too hot and then too cold. Soon you'll stagger back into the dining room with your cigarette and she'll giggle, because it'll be a ten foot spliff full of sweet and sour sauce and colorful chunks of bell pepper. If you do get this far, for Pete's sake be careful when you light the thing or you'll wind up scorching the antique dining table.

A LONG WAY FROM HELL

Jeremy Sellers

Satan stood outside the Chapel, snuffing a Camel into the sidewalk with his boot, hot smoke rolling from his nostrils. He arched his back, flexing the trapezius muscles, causing his wings to smooth against broad, naked shoulders as he attempted to navigate the doorway. Inside this holy place a group of his peers awaited the leader of their Bible Studies class. Three new students sat at *his* pew. "Move," he barked, throwing a head-nod toward the back of the room. Without question, the three kids grabbed their stuff and scurried to safety. Satan dumped his book-bag on the floor and poured himself into the pew. Raking talon-like fingers through hair so gold its radiance could bleach the eyes of observers, he found a *vanity* mirror at the bottom of his pack.

Angela entered the room. Her scent was upon him instantly. As her graceful form floated closer, Satan became erect, but she wouldn't flash a smile. Their eyes met. She snatched her glance from his. Nose up, she quickened the pace toward her pew.

"Hey, big guy," Michael spoke from behind, tapping Satan's wing. "That's quite an apple."

Satan's head spun around, his eyes dark and jewel-like. "God knows why she'll have nothing to do with me. I'm beautiful."

"Ah, here-in lies the problem," Michael shook his finger. "The key to picking this girl's locks is dropping the attitude. These chicks don't dig the hubris."

"I haven't felt lust like this since I sought the throne of God. Must I be deprived of those things I most covet, perpetually?" Satan groaned.

"Something else to consider, try leaving the baggage in the past. Catholic girls are a little weary of rebel angels."

"But the things they say about Catholic girls in hell," Satan insisted.

"Myths."

"Ah, *strigas et fictos lupus credere.*" Satan's nostrils flared.

"Yeah, witches, politicians, telephone psychics. They can make us wolves believe anything." Michael smiled. "But listen, I'm here to score, too. Stick with me. We'll work on your game."

EL AMOR: A STORY BEGINNING IN SPANISH

Judith Ortiz Cofer

Dos palomas en la ventana—two doves cooing and fluttering their wings on the window ledge draw me away from my work to witness the little drama unfolding below: a man in black pacing outside a café, smoking a cigarette he holds between thumb and index finger, inhaling deeply once, twice, *un gran suspiro,* then crushing it balletically under the toe of the black mirror of his shoe. He smells his hands, runs his fingers through pomaded hair, lights another. He glances at his watch. He does not yet see her moving in slow, seductive *bolero* tempo towards him. Red dress, red purse, red mouth—substantial hips and ass, hard little cones of breasts pointing straight ahead—a body strong and firm as any promise made by any woman to any man in the entire history of sex, she is a pendulum in tune with the turning of the world. On first sight of his *destino*, his body tenses like that of a Flamenco dancer poised to stomp his way into her *corazón.* Her pace slows even more under his gaze, her hips and purse synchronizing their swing and sway. Then, tossing her glossy mane, smoothing down her dress over her curves, five paces away, she stops. *¿Entonces, que pasa, amigos?* Propelled forward by a command he thinks comes straight from his heart—but, friends, it was scripted into his cells long before he knew he would be born a man, not just any man, but *el hombre,* the one destined to possess this *mujer*—he grabs her arm, they lock steps, and exit my field of vision. I sway over space trying to see what happens next, nearly losing my grasp and frightening the *palomas,* which soar off into the darkening sky, one in close pursuit of the other. And I am caught in the moment, *el instante, amigos,* when any story, in any language, anywhere in the world, may begin, at any time; suspended *aquí*— somewhere between desire and death.

THE ARMS OF A GOOD WOMAN

Judith Ortiz Cofer

Although he has been away too long this time, and a foreign smell may still be clinging to him—he knows she is sensitive to this—she lets him in, draws a warm bath scented with Verbena, Bloodroot, and Rue; herbs from the thriving garden she tends in a small plot outside her kitchen. He likes hearing her say their names in her own tongue, and she does so as she pours the water over him like a blessing: *Azafrán, Enebro, Mandrágora, and Nenúfar.* Afterwards, she anoints his whole body with oil, offers to cut his hair grown long and wild—he can't refuse the lure of her knowing hands—the blade's run on the back of his neck sending shivers through him as in sex—making them both laugh aloud. Kneeling, she takes his traveling feet into her hands, trims his hard-as-horn toenails—silver scissors cool against his skin. She kisses the tender spot between his ankle and heel. He feels the gentle pressure of her teeth and thinks of shells he has stepped on at the beach—strange how vulnerable he feels with her kneeling at his feet. He has to smile, watching her gather up each strand of hair and nail clipping from the floor. She wraps the commas and little crescent moons like gifts in scraps of paper he recognizes as lines torn from a poem or prayer, before placing them over a candle's small flame. For a moment, he is alarmed by the smell of singed flesh, but as she slips into their bed, folding herself perfectly into his body's curve, he breathes in only the familiar jasmine on her skin, a scent she mixes herself just to please him. *Such a peculiar woman*, he thinks. But he is an understanding man, and she loves him like no other. He is too tired for lovemaking just then, and of course, she understands. He soon surrenders to a deep and easy sleep, cradled in the fragrant arms of a good woman.

THE WORST UNIVERSITY EVER

Ben Percy

It is the worst university ever. Everyone agrees.

Last April, *U.S. News and World Report* published a special "Worst Universities" issue. This place blew the competition out of the water. It made the other worst universities look just golden. When asked how he felt about their status, the Dean said, "We are clearly the worstest."

The Worst University Ever has no president, no provost, no vice chancellor of student affairs. There is only the Dean. The Dean's first name is Dean. Everyone finds this terrifically ironic. It is often joked about during cocktail parties and faculty meetings. "I was born to be a dean," Dean Dean says, prodding people with his elbow.

There is something about the Dean that cannot be trusted. One student remarked, "He laughs like a pedophile."

The Dean stages an annual Halloween riot because he believes it engenders school spirit. He also appreciates the publicity. He kindles a bonfire where straw effigies dressed up in Harvard and Yale sweatshirts are ceremoniously lynched, then burned.

The Dean hosts a special lecture every semester: "What I've Learned So Far." No one ever goes. Sometimes not even the Dean.

When the students fulfill their major requirements, they're called into the Dean's office. He pumps their hand and says, "Good for you, you son of a B." Then there is the bill. Visa is the only credit card accepted at The Worst University Ever. There is no graduation ceremony, no diploma. Just the trip to Dean Dean's office. Before he wishes you a fond farewell, he might ask you to play horsey on his knee. Or he might not. In the end, you get a plastic union card and set off into the real world with your shoulders square, your chin held high with pride and optimism.

HUNGER

Virgil Suarez

Someone brings up a cow again, the idea of it chewing cud absentmindedly by the side of the highway. We are sitting here in the dark gnashing our teeth, our empty mouths hollow and bitter with silence. Our stomachs grumbling.

We never speak of bread, not even to joke, not even to say: "if only I had a piece of bread, I —" Nothing here but cobwebs and lint in our pockets.

Where are we? You ask.

We are on the edge of hunger, we like to say, our self-consumption like our belief in a God of internal combustion. Any minute now will cease this craving.

CUBAN DREAM #7

Virgil Suarez

I'm on the beach running after a red parasol, each time I get near, a gust blows it down—it goes over German & Italian tourists, tumbling, kicking up sand into their drinks. They shout: *"Ragazzo! Achtung!"* A red umbrella in the distance, a knotted-tendril medusa of all my dreams—I run after it & step atop dead urchin carcasses. Unseen needles spear my soles, prick deep like lost loves. *Puas,* as my father called these urchins, these pains, warning me to steer clear. I leave blood tracks in the sand, beaded gems of my passing.

A woman wants to know if I can help her reenact Ava Gardner's scene in *The Night of the Iguana,* the one with the two heavily-tanned boys who sandwich the star in the sultry Acapulco night. Pepe shakes his maracas. The other, the nameless one, dances behind Ava, arms linked tight about her waist. So shocking for 50s America. I say she's got the wrong country. I say she's got the wrong idea.

The umbrella becomes a speck, a small dot my father's ghost plucks out of the air & puts in his mouth. I've gone deaf. I don't even hear the waves, then sound becomes possible again. Waves hiss. Sand churns. I hear the roar of the surf. I hear someone behind me calling for another *mojito,* this island's minty-fresh elixir! In the distance my father's ghost has become a raft in a rough-&-tumble sea: women & children fall overboard, splash in the water. Drown. Nobody notices. I turn to look behind me only to see a beach covered in blue umbrellas & under their shades thousands of naked German women, their waxen skin turning beet red. They are hungry seals. One hobbles over to me & begins to gnaw at my shins. Her bite feels like a clamping down of metal into flesh, the smashing of a finger under a hammerblow. It does no good to shout for help, or to try to wake up. This is the lost dream of a lost soul in a distant but not forgotten island.

THE CYCLIST

Janice Eidus

Once, not so long ago, everything would have appeared beautiful to you: grass, birds, blue sky, trees.

But today you sit in the park, unable to see past the darkness of your thoughts. The doctors say that your moods "cycle"; they call you a "cyclist." Like a bicyclist, you think: proud, high, and cocksure on the seat one moment, tumbling to the ground the next.

Certainly you know the drill: when you fall, you must immediately rise, dust yourself off, laugh at your clumsiness, and climb right back up on that seat. But what if one day you don't want to get up? What if the dirt and mud in which you lie feel like all that you have ever known, all that you will ever deserve? What if you truly believe that the world would be a better place if you returned to the soil from which you sprang?

What if you have completely given up on the pills the doctors gave you, the pills that caused you so much agony and didn't help? What if you think constantly of Sylvia Plath and Anne Sexton; of the jazz singer you knew who recently jumped from a high-rise window?

What if, as you lie there, tasting the dark clotted earth, you fantasize about how you'll do it: pills; razor blade; oven; plastic bag ...? What then?

Well, here's what you will do: you will rise from the ground, dust yourself off, laugh like a fool, and climb right back up on that bicycle seat. You will embrace the beauty of grass, birds, blue sky, and trees. They are yours once again, and you are theirs.

BLACK CAT

Josh Russell

Remember prom, boutonniere pressed flat as if it'd been preserved in a book. Remember heat radiating through rented pants, through creaking tulle skirts, more than the heat of first sex. Remember blood on the sheet, the twitch of pleasure that shook her. Remember college, Saturday nights becoming Sunday mornings, coffee and the *Post* in bed, comics and front page kicked to the floor, sliding and crashing like water. Remember the breakup. Remember hours of pool with Physics major sharps who could not lose. Remember running into her at Sibbie's party senior year. Remember being naked in the Honda in the parking lot, rain like code on the roof, windows fogging, then glowing as dawn broke. Remember the Christmas tree blown into the middle of the street in which the black cat played. Remember laughing at her while she stood at the second story window clad only in a blanket conversing in Spanish with Mormons, too polite to ignore the bell. Remember the months during which the only reasons you wanted to see each other were to fuck and have your papers proofread. Remember driving away to Baton Rouge, long lists of vows trailing. Remember the second breakup. Remember sadness and loneliness like possessions taking up space in the room. Remember your birthday falling on Thanksgiving, the trip north, how she gave herself like a gift. Remember Christmas. Remember the night she begged to be taken back and you, standing barefoot on the tiny rusted landing, looking at the alley's luminous shell gravel and listening to her voice being pulled thin by a thousand miles of fiber optics, sure that prospects for love were numerous in that weird city, said no.

"WINTER ON FIFTH AVENUE, NEW YORK"

Josh Russell

Stieglitz stands in a snowstorm for three hours, moustache a comb of frost, waiting for the moment. Fifth Avenue is crossed with cart tracks. The borrowed camera he holds, a 4 x 5-inch detective, is capable of only a single shot. Children in scarves pass and he spies on them, but they are too small. Two workmen shovel a sidewalk. A glazier's wagon passes, frozen glass rattling. A man's derby flies from his head. There have been arguments, a scuffle even, over the worth of the hand camera. Samuel Leone claims it is too coarse for art, too simple. He demands a tripod, a huge negative. This horizontally-blown snow, this avenue with its wheelruts and gas lamps, this city of burning coal and horses with smoking breath, Stieglitz knows, will prove Leone wrong. The window of a nearby café is curtained by condensation. Above the wind's howl there is a noise like a pistol shot. It is the whip of a man driving his team—the ice delivery, product made useless by February. When he prints the picture Stieglitz will crop away more than half of the image. He steps into the team's path.

In the warm café his ears sting and his toes tingle as his boots thaw on the planks. Stieglitz has wrapped the camera inside his scarf, and he drinks chocolate, bending over it to warm his nose. His moustache melts, shedding drops of water into his mug. The café is empty except for Stieglitz and a man who wipes the tops of vacant tables with a rag. Stieglitz takes his eyes away from the chocolate and watches. Diffused light spills over the man. The rag has been cut from the cloth of a dress and its pattern is alive in his hand.

BAD SLAW, BAD KARMA, BADASS

Michael Griffith

I'll tell it straight, friend: how I turned badass. My pop and I were going in—this was Kansas City, a rib joint, picnic tables on a cement slab slanted toward drains so it could be hosed down at night, peppery grease on the ribs, the walls, the body-shop calendars; the kind of place where every guy had a napkin big as a manhole cover wedged in his collar—we were ten feet from the door when we ran into Nixon. It was the late '70s, before people forgot what a scuzzy old wardheeler Tricky Dick was. The crook had a big dab of sauce on the end of his nose.

We tried to be nice. My pop grinned and flicked a finger and said, "Might want to give the old beak a wiperoo, Mr. President." Nixon didn't reach for a hankie, didn't smile, didn't ball up his fist or bomb Cambodia or have Gordon Liddy feed us our livers.

"Good cole slaw," he announced. "*Good* cole slaw." His jowls looked damp with pork juice; his monobrow wagged solemnly. I was just a kid—I believed him; I believed *in* him.

Pop nudged me, and we went in.

As if he hadn't done enough already, the son of a bitch lied. The slaw was rancid, like pale kelp adrift in a pool of souring milk. I hated it. Listen to me: I'm what happens when a boy loses faith; I'm what happens when you're sold on foul slaw by the one-time leader of the free world. Point the finger where you will, friend—I *know* what rot of the soul, what failure of human kindness, what false witness landed me in here. It was never the same, my life. How could it have been? Ain't nothing pollutes a man like rancid cabbage, blinky horseradish, pickle brine gone bad. Ain't nothing.

DISSONANT, HURTFUL, AND HERS

Michael Griffith

On the tray beside her is a glass of papaya juice, iced; she's made him garnish it, grumblingly, with a bright wheel of orange. On the chintz arm of the easy chair, the remote control. Behind her a stack of fashion magazines, fresh from their vacu-wrappers, providing lumbar support and, if she gets around to it, reading material. She's constructed a wobbly tower of throw pillows, and her swollen foot, swathed in gauze, perches atop it like a pasha. She's waited twenty years for this; she can hear him upstairs, tidying. The low roar of discontent, or is it the vacuum? A thrill to listen: The drone of the machine gets louder when he lifts it off the floor, again and again and again, to go over a sly speck of dirt that won't—just won't, just won't—come up; she hears the whining fade when, straying out of range, he rips the cord from its socket. In the bedroom, a week's worth of pennies and toothpicks and paperclips rattles up the wand. Serves him right. He's doing the area around his bedside table, where he daily dumps his pocket oddments and never stoops to retrieve what rolls away. She can hear him curse: They sound like gunshots, the coins sucked into the vacuum's angry maw. She can hear him grunt, see him jump back in surprise with every fearsome copper-rattle. Her machine, her martyr. When she glances down at her foot, it's swaying from side to side, despite the damaged ankle, as though keeping time to some tune she can't name. It's a tune she likes: dissonant, hurtful, and hers.

APPETITES

Sharon Wahl

I woke up in the mood for pecan waffles and maple syrup and spicy fennel sausages. I like to eat. What doesn't? So why not, I thought, make a meal for everything?

I spent the day scattering bread, sunflower seeds, sesame seeds, millet. I caught bugs and fed them to the lizards. I let the earwigs in the hummingbird feeder loose in their own pool of nectar. I fed mice to the snakes and owls, rabbits to the bobcats. I fed peanuts to the mice and gophers and woodrats. That's how I caught them.

But that's what they would have eaten anyway, you might say. Well yes, but everything was thoughtfully prepared. When I fed the coyotes their squirrels, for example, I first removed some of the less digestible bits—tails, feet and claws, little teeth—then soaked them in a nice sauce.

I fed catfood to the bluejays. They love it. I fed hay to the cows, extra hay to the nursing ones. The pregnant cows I fed by hand, holding handfuls of straw up to their mouths so they wouldn't need to bend over. It is big enough being a cow without having another cow crammed inside of you. And all day, I kept pots of water boiling on the stove, making clouds of steam to feed the wind. The doors and windows were wide open and I could see him tasting it, the vapor rising and shifting direction. Fresh sweet clouds, scented with rosewater. Delicious.

THE NANNIES GATHER TO STUDY THE STARS

Chauna Craig

They're all out of high school, just, and fueled by the stories whispered at agencies, how one lucky girl was discovered while diapering an actor's baby. A director stopped by and some curve of her lip, the coo of her voice, sold him. *Who? Who?* And any name is uttered with the same result: awe and, on the dotted line, another name each hopes will be worth millions.

In Hollywood, these nannies gather some nights, support group dreamed up by an agency, only it's not about homesickness for Wyoming or Maine, but connections. They study the homes of the stars for clues: brands of dishes, clothes they now borrow and will someday buy. The nanny for the minor soap star laments how she decided against a producer's triplets. With her legs she could have starred in his latest thriller.

Finally one of them becomes famous. She makes the paper when her SUV spins out of control on Receda, killing her and a notoriously difficult director's boys. The nannies gather and occupy themselves with details like what flowers he sent to her family. *White orchids of course, she said he always sends orchids. Why would he send anything for the girl that killed his family? Because he's got class, that's why.*

Then, nibbling low-fat cookies, each imagines how, if her obscurity continues to cling like an odor, she too can drive crazy and leave behind a small but faithful club to borrow black Armani and tell how this tragedy was inevitable.

STARLIGHT

Robert McGovern

Her back was up against me and it was sliding down my chest and her hands were at the nape of my neck and I could barely breathe and I only wanted to touch her fingers or elbow or other elbow or chin or lower lobe of either ear and I was trying not to look directly into the light of her skin but I did and I was blinded and she whispering from some cosmos of the private room:

Twinkle, twinkle, little star, how I wonder how big you are.

My friend had brought me to Mustang Sally's. He thought I was having a nervous breakdown. He even paid for my therapy session with Star.

I didn't think a lap dance was going to help.

A few seconds into the song, Star banged her elbow into my forehead. She kissed it. "I'm sorry, honey. I just started a couple weeks ago. Haven't worked out the kinks." Her breath shined against my ear.

I decided I was going to touch her. Risk the heat. Try to match her speed of light and catch it. Maybe glow for a few seconds in the dark.

I wish I may, I wish I might.

We had to be made of the same substance—starlight, and I needed her to bring it out of the immovable crust and rock that sat on the couch under her. I was a pilgrim searching for a star to guide me through the night.

My index finger started to orbit her skin like a clumsy Sputnik. I could feel the heat through my body; my skin started to gleam the closer I got to her with my finger. I hoped we would expand beyond ourselves and collapse onto the floor and merge into one celestial body and burn out forever.

Starlight was nursing me past human purview. I was becoming universal.

But the song was over. She stood up and smiled. "Time's up, honey." And the expanse of myself went dim.

DEBRIS

Kit Coyne Irwin

As Coralee spun inside the tornado, her baby was ripped from her arms. She looked for her amid the swirling cows, sheet metal, and autoparts, but couldn't see her. An old hand eggbeater blew past, its handle churning. Coralee knew tornadoes don't keep what they take. The tornado spat her out, into a drainage ditch along state road 141. Two days later the nurse told her that her daughter had been found unharmed in the middle of a wheat field. "Found her sitting in one of them recliners. Naughahyde. Can you imagine?" Coralee got to keep the chair, and found it was leather, buttery leather. Now whenever Coralee and her daughter hear the siren, they climb into the chair, pull back on the solid wood handle. Their feet raise up, their backs recline. They are ready for their ride.

BLACK RIVERS

Melissa Gurley Bancks

Lavinia fills her front porch rocker like air fills a balloon, and Lord is she sweating, great black rivers of sweat and flesh singing in this heat. It's so hot she can't cook in the kitchen, so cousin Mike is using the front yard grille, that molasses and brown sugar soaking up the fire like Lavinia fills up her chair.

Sweet clouds of hickory steam swallow Mike's face. His spatula's on fire, great hissing flames kissing that silver. It's so beautiful here, with all my cousins running in the sprinkler and the sun turning everything orange, and Lavinia lording over everything from her rocker thump-thumping concrete. From Lavinia's house here on the hill, we can see the steam covered Mississippi rolling along, it's chocolate taking on the color of the sunset. I close my eyes and picture my shadow stretching long as that river winds.

It doesn't matter here, not today anyway, that I'm the one nobody wanted when God stole my parents. Lavinia says they were all too scared to take me cause I looked too much like Mama (and I do, I've checked the pictures). She said looking at me was like seeing Mama's ghost, but Lavinia isn't afraid of ghosts, so she took me and I grew in her kitchen and other rooms of her house. And today all this blackness surrounds me like I'm rolling in jewels. Boys from the senior high are driving by with their bmp-bmp-bmp, cars trembling with all that bass. Everything is glowing tangerine.

Still, Lavinia says when my curves come, everything will change. But right now Mike's hands are on fire and the sugar crusted chicken is baking sweet, and up there Lavinia is laughing, her chair thump-thumping music like the barges moving slow down black rivers.

UNLIKELY MAGIC

Melissa Gurley Bancks

They picked grass to fill mattresses, slept together on the floor after the bank took the farm, all the hogs gone to cholera. When even the chickens joined the conspiracy, their egg shells so weak, the whites would seep through, Great-Grandma Mary fed her hungry birds ground glass mixed with seed; with a rock from the garden, she pounded her fine wedding china to powder, scattered the dust in the feed.

Three generations later, under a sun already red with heat, the air heavy, I find myself cooing to my grandmother's chickens in the coop. Disturbed by the skin-like thinness of the eggs I collect, she sends me on a mission.

So there I am, northern accent flattening my syllables in an Arkansas feed store, spilling my rapid tale of ground glass to a patient man behind the counter, a bartender the way he listens, used to diagnosing sight unseen.

The floor's so thick with dust my shoes have carved a crooked pattern to the counter. This old man's knuckles are red as the patches in his cheeks. Not even flinching an eyelid, he assures me oyster shells are what I need to get those chickens laying thick-shelled eggs, my story apparently not so sensational.

So I pay the dollars, carry the shells like silver beads back to the house, the coop, scatter this unlikely magic in their food. Within a week, the brown skin is so thick on those eggs, they crack in even halves, the yolks perfect gold suns inside.

They are golden as Great Grandma Mary's necklace I wear down low beneath my blouse, aware sometimes of how it presses, like a book, like a Bible between my breasts.

#3

Ben Miller

She wanted to be a teacher, a very good teacher, and could think of no better way to begin than to gag and blindfold her tiny brother and then pour ice-cold water on his wrists. He would be Helen Keller. She would be everything else.

BOYS AND GIRLS WILL BE MEN

Marilyn Krysl

Draw a tight circle around it. Sit on it. Put a rock on it. Put another rock on the rock on it. Sit on the rocks. Remove rocks, stamp on it with both feet. Stand on top of it and perform a ritual act, Abraham with his sword raised above Isaac. Stand on top of it and salute the flag of maniacal cheerfulness. Stand on top of it and salute the flag of tonnage, the flag of traffic potential. The flag of six figures. The flag of Better Living through Missing Children.

Put some weights on it, lay asphalt over the weights. Construct a mall over the asphalt. Stack the mall with petroleum products. Put a fundraiser on it, put a crowd pleaser on it, put a brick freight train on it. Add several tankers of dead elephant meat. Now stand on it. Eschew buoyancy.

Slice it into thinner and thinner strips. Vitrify the strips. Put a stadium on the vitrified strips. Throw a bowl game. Get little boys to throw little bowl games. Add attentive mothers wearing short shorts made in Barundi for Claymore. This is the new pornography, but don't call it that. Don't call it the death of beauty. Don't call it cannon fodder. Call up Homeland Security in case there's a sniper in it, but don't call it by its name.

Now look: up through the compacted autobodies something is sprouting. This thing has a vermilion sunset; it's flying a kite over the general's vault. It's got an aria, it's got an avalanche, there's a pie in its enemy's face. There's a hawk soaring above it. You thought it was the spirit of individualism rising up through the muck of commerce? Look again.

It's got a string quartet in its hair and blood on its hands.

PRETTY HEART

Kathleen McGookey

Pretty heart, my doctor says, looking at the ultrasound monitor. I want to know if it is whole, alarmed already by what science has told me precisely: the baby's weight and sex and brain size . . . and statistical chances of terrible defects. Today we see his tongue move, inside his mouth, inside me, his own small ocean. Cross-sectioned (*like if you cut a salami in half,* the sonographer explains), the heart's four small dark circles, marbles, miniature moons, bluebird eggs—that fragile?—the flutters quick, irregular. I recognize it when they point it out: pretty. I hope she means it's formed the way it should. I don't want to hear about real trouble—babies whose heads or hearts don't grow, or grow wrong, instead of this pretty one we've got. Suddenly, I can't say it, can't ask, *what if?* Can't ask—those babies—their hearts—*The initial test results,* my doctor says, *don't change.* I can't think. Instead I'm seeing wallpaper, blue blankets, blue moons, weighing luck and science, in unequal doses, with our baby's new socks, arranged in his dresser for months, waiting in darkness, small and secret, like he is, like we are.

JOE

Kathleen McGookey

We take the boy with one leg out in our boat. That he has one leg is not his fault: no accident or lapse, just bad luck. He throws his crutches in the truck, hops, then grabs his friend's baseball cap. I've met him twice. Today's his grace: he balances on one ski around the lake, around the only other boat, a family fishing, who nearly drop their poles and stare: a one-legged boy, did you see that? A contraption held up with ropes and mirrors, wind and light. Seen from another angle, it's the same imperfect picture: he grins. He's playing. I don't ask, *do you think about dying?* How stupid of me, how gloom and doom. He watches for girls in bikinis. We're all dying. That's one way of thinking: the foghorn's deep groan can't rescue us, lost in our boats. But in the noon sun of Saturday, he's blonde and tan and lanky, the picture of sixteen, so far from how he began: a tiny package, rosy and sleepy, ten fingers, ten toes.

SIXTH GRADE

Janet Wondra

Children, today we will learn to spell assassination, a-s-s, a-s-s, i-n; a-s-s, a-s-s, i-n-a-t-e; a-s-s, a-s-s, i-n-a, t-i-o-n. A whole family of words—the person, the action, the thing.

Watch the TV. See how the Spanish lesson is interrupted. That's i-n-t-e-, double r, u-p-t-e-d. We don't know what's happening yet. The President is shot. We must wait patiently. That's spelled the same as patient in a hospital. We must wait like sick people. No, the President is not sick, he's deceased. We spelled that last week. Now watch the pictures. There has been an assassination. It's like Mississippi—two sets of double s's. A-s-s, a-s-s, i-n-a, t-i-o-n.

Watch as the bullet hits him. Watch as the men run towards the car. Watch as Jackie climbs over the trunk, some say to rescue the top of the President's head, some say deserting her husband. Now, watch again as the President is shot.

Here is the assassin, a-s-s, a-s-s, i-n. Again, those double s's like Mississippi. Here is an assassin assassinating the assassin. See, once you know a word, all the time you find ways to use it. When you grow up you may want to join the Army. If you like codes, you may do very well. Even if you don't, you'll read the newspaper, and every morning you'll remember this lesson.

THREE-LEGGED DOGS

Jane Armstrong

In a single day, I had these encounters with dogs who were missing a leg:

1. On my way to work, I noticed in the yard of a house down the street from me a golden retriever, balanced like a tripod camera, intently watching as my car passed his domain.

2. Walking downtown during my lunch hour, I saw a handmade sign tacked to a community bulletin board: LOST. OLD ENGLISH SHEEPDOG. FOUR YEARS OLD. WEARING RED BANDANA AND MISSING RIGHT FRONT LEG. The poster featured a photocopied picture of the wayward pet.

3. From my office window, I watched as a lady strolled down the sidewalk with her three-legged standard poodle. The poodle, managing quite nicely, hopped along, unconscious of its handicap.

I thought it odd, so many incomplete dogs living in one small town. They must always have been here. I wondered what had become of the amputated limbs. I imagined them existing, somewhere, apart from their former hosts. On windy nights, the rigid legs click together like *tinickling* sticks. When the moon is full and bright, the limbs rise up into the air and land back down, one upon the other, in sets of three, in magical and suggestive patterns.

I am forty-seven years old and until this day, I had never seen a three-legged dog.

In much the same way, names will be revealed to me. And faces.

OCTOBER

Keith Scribner

Showing her around his city—the coffee place with worn velvet couches, the restaurant that makes its own caramel, the park with sculpture lit up at night—he has been looking through her, she thinks, barely seeing her beside the Minerva bronze and its long flaming shadows, stopping mid-sentence in his memories, so as she follows a waiter between tight tables in his favorite Indian restaurant, burned Tandoori and a sitar note hanging in the air, she's not surprised when she turns and finds he has stopped halfway back to the door where small gift-wrapped boxes sit on a table between three women, one of whom she recognizes from his old photos, wavy blond hair and bright lipstick, Clara, reaching for him, her palms turned up, shiny red and yellow bangles rattling down her wrists, saying, "Davey, you remember," and he says through a smile, "Your birthday. Ten-ten. How could I forget?"

FLAT ON MY BACK

Gary Fincke

My second night on the job, hearing my father take orders from a boss who cursed him, I was ashamed, staying in the gym I was cleaning until he'd bowed his head to lift and carry a shipment of lined tablets and spiral notebooks.

Soundless, flat on my back, I slid under the bleachers to scrape gum and snot. My father, the janitor who had begged this summer-home-from-college job for me, carried those cartons three-high, passing the door thirty-two times.

Summer was when the high school recovered from injuries, but that evening carved its initials in the air, spray-painted the *eat-me* and *fuck-you* of contempt. Tiny obscenities were inked in the spaces between the bleachers' wood slats—three ways to enter Courtney, ten ways to kill Mr. Wallace, and the one thing the tiniest printer wanted to do again and again to Mrs. Kane. I made those stories smear and disappear. I was sure my father's boss, after I punched out, would inspect my work with a mirror on a stick, grading like a dentist.

In the lobby, an hour later, my father was taking fingerprints from windows as if every student was a suspect, as if he expected something from the mathematics of work besides division and subtraction. By eleven, everything heavy looked like something I wanted to throw through glass. The moist, outside air hissed dares until my father squealed that row of windows clean. And then my father, dragging a mop from a bucket on wheels, put a DO NOT ENTER sign in the door I looked through and switched off the lobby lights before he began to swing from side to side toward the sullen night.

THE PROGRESS OF DAYS

Gabriel Welsch

My sister Wanda cried on the phone, of love lost—ten years ago that day her Bill sped over a sudden ice patch, black on the asphalt—and her pitch and sheer duration meant she was off her medication. I don't know which one—no one could keep track of the bright pills in the sky-blue plastic boxes with the abbreviations for days of the week embossed on seven pop-up lids, a sequence entirely dependent on a moment of lucidity, late on a Sunday evening, when Wanda would sit at her kitchen table, pill jars lined up on the faux-marble Formica, and fill each of the blue boxes with daily dosages so that her mornings could begin as they should, reaching for the boxes next to the pothos vine creeping across the kitchen sill, the terminal leaf digging at the pane to meet the outside beyond the casement glass, among the air shared by dogs, shrubbery, and exhaust, where the grass came and went over her husband's grave, where foot tracks wore paths among the stones and smoothed moguls of the dead—where I would walk when she finished talking, or tired herself out so she had to sit among her clivias, her pots of peace lily and ivy with curled tendrils and narrowing leaves, and I would check the mail, look for the misguided optimism of a sign, whatever that meant, and I would see only the surly crow that haunts our street—and recall Wanda saying that crows are absurd, the absurdists of the avian world, death in flight—and the crow hung from a tree limb, crumbs sifting from his beak, ready to drop on an unsuspecting dog, and I would curse her fate, curse the crow, wonder why we are forced to choose our signs.

HERO

Jotham Burrello

Jiha rolls the bloodstained poker under the train platform as the men pass tobacco and drink between their coal-marked hands. Its shiny tip haunts him.

Jiha had led the parade through their village. The poker led them. It spun high in the air. The miners knew Jiha was a brute, the strongest in the pit, but they never expected the pink-cheeked boy to lead them.

"Student radicals, neo-fascist anarchists, desecrating your capital," said the President-elect in his radio plea. "Who's loyal to the motherland?" he exclaimed, then promised to find the miners' back wages.

In the city, produce trucks stocked with truncheons or rubber-hoses delivered them to the protester's tent-city. Police officials smoked nearby.

The student hid under a newspaper kiosk. The miners smelled his urine. Jiha raised the poker over his head like a dagger, the gold handle gleaming. The plywood kiosk flipped easily. Jiha shut his eyes.

Coming down with the poker Jiha remembered a fable about a man who had lived with a rail spike rooted in his skull. "It split his gray matter," the elders reported. "He fathered nine children."

Finally the poker stopped crashing. A miner dropped his club. Blood streamed down the student's face but he was conscious. He fingered the poker then gripped its shaft with both hands. Perhaps he'd heard the fable.

Jiha vomited. His shoulders knifed-back, jerking the poker up; its barbed hook prying out the student's brain through the pie-shaped slit in his skull.

On the platform the supervisor raises Jiha's arm and the men cheer. He reenacts the fatal blow and the men laugh. He inspects the bone fragments frozen to the spike. A man whistles.

Jiha snatches the poker, unsettling the supervisor's helmet. He runs toward an approaching train scraping the poker down the platform. Small sparks fly.

THE KING OF MINIMUM WAGE

Jose Chavez

At eighteen I landed a job at a turkey joint, hose blastin' gravy from tin cups, a clean-cut kid in a blue Tam-O-Shanter cap. Crazy Tony worked the grill and ran the show like a renegade Messiah, slipping us slices of roast beef and ham on the sly cuz, he said, "you gotta stick it to the Man, whenever you can."

Friday nights slammed with old folks in hair nets and cowboy boots, the kitchen's hot as chicken grease and orders spun like a roulette wheel. Crazy Tony sang golden oldies to boost morale, belting doo-wops and shooby-doos with seven orders up, dish tub busting a gut, his hands like freight trains. He re-told jokes until they were funny and—God forbid—when there was a lull, sculpted naked women from mashed potatoes, dressed up turkeys to look like celebrities.

We all though *he* was the Man, till one night Crazy Tony went too far: he stuck a carrot out the belt of his apron like a boner, then started doin' an Elvis number, singin' into a raw turkey leg like a microphone. All hell broke loose: a waitress screamed, a busboy fainted and before Crazy Tony knew what hit him, the ax had come down as sure as sunset, and our Savior was walkin' silently out the back door, his white apron hanging over his shoulders like a cape.

CLASS REPORT

Brent Spencer

At the age of eight, he gave a class report called "My Dad Died." The climax—actually, the whole story was climax—was a dramatic mid-air collision between his father's jet fighter and a double-decker passenger plane. He'd made drawings to illustrate. The one where everyone died in a winged fireball went over especially well. His teacher gave him both a gold star and a face with one pendulous tear, drawn free-hand because that's the kind of teacher she was. The story did not go over well at home, not with his father, anyway, who didn't know if he was more offended by the wished-for death or by the foolishness of the death. He wasn't even sure if this was a punishable offense. In the week or so before his actual death, he thought about his son's strange story day and night. All thinking stopped the day he laid his 747 on its side, peeling the skin of the plane all the way to the bone.

DOWN IN THE JUNGLE ROOM

Brent Spencer

Alejandro Contreras but you probably know me as Buddy Savage. No? Esta bien. Call me Alé. I was the Mexican Tarzan. At night mostly, our company would use the sets the gringo Tarzan used during the day. I swung from the same vines. I wrestled the same lions. All in good Castillian. A conquistador in a loincloth. Our natives were mostly played by indios, you see. That's called "theme." I got to like that loincloth a little too much, if you want to know. This pinché city. I tried to give them the house for a museum, but no. I'm not famous enough. Twenty-three movies and the bottom fell out of the Tarzan business. I made a few detective movies. Sometimes, as a confidence builder, I wore my loincloth under my detective pants, but it didn't help. Nobody wanted to see me as anything but Tarzan, and nobody wanted to see Tarzan. Now I'm going to live with my daughter. Once I swung through the trees and now she worries I'll trip on the carpeting. Sucks to be me, as my grandson says. Sometimes he and I get stoned and watch the old movies. I'm not proud of that, but I'm not ashamed of it either.

THE CUSTODIAN

Brian Hinshaw

The job would get boring if you didn't mix it up a little. Like this woman in 14-A, the nurses called her the mockingbird, start any song and this old lady would sing it though. Couldn't speak, couldn't eat a lick of solid food, but she sang like a house on fire. So for a kick, I would go in there with my mop and such, prop the door open with bucket, and set her going. She was best at songs you'd sing with a group—"Oh Susanna," campfire stuff. Any kind of Christmas song worked good too, and it always cracked the nurses if I could get her into "Let It Snow" during a heat spell. We'd try to make her take up a song from the radio or some the old songs with cursing in them, but she would never go for those. Although once I had her do "How Dry I Am" while Nurse Winchell fussed with the catheter.

Yesterday, her daughter or maybe granddaughter comes in while 14-A and I were partways into "Auld Lang Syne" and the daughter says "oh oh oh" like she had interrupted scintillating conversation and then she takes a long look at 14-A there in the gurney with her eyes shut and her curled-up hands, taking a cup of kindness yet. And the daughter looks at me the way a girl does at the end of an old movie and she says, "my god," says, "you're an angel," and now I can't do it anymore, can hardly step into the room.

HORSE HEAVY

Lori Ann Stephens

Ella's daddy used to sing us to sleep. Tuck us in like hot tamales and sing about a spooky girl.

> *She came in so tired and weary,*
> *and she went upstairs to bed.*
> *Put her false teeth upon the mantle,*
> *her cork leg under the bed.*
> *Put her glass eye on the window*
> *and she hung up her blonde hair.*
> *My little girl you know I love you*
> *but you're scattered everywhere.*

Ella's daddy had a big back, so big we both climbed on, Ella and me. We'd rub until his back was all bread dough of hair and freckles.

I waited alone for Ella on the prickly couch, Ella's daddy reading the newspaper.

"I owe you a rub," he said. "Hop on the floor."

Ella's daddy's hands rubbed my arms, back, behind, legs. He turned me over, and whispered shhhh. His prickly mustache and brown earthworm eyes looked down at me, and his sweaty fingers crawled under my shirt. My arms, legs, head scattered everywhere.

"Isn't Ella coming home soon?" I choked.

"Relax," he said.

The kitchen telephone rang. Ring. Ring. Ring.

"Won't you get it?"

Ring. Ring. Ring. His fingers, horse heavy, moved up under my shirt.

Ring. Ring. Ring.

"Stay here," Ella's daddy said. He galloped to the phone.

I raced to the bathroom and locked it shut.

I looked at the spooky girl in the mirror. Her nostrils flared wild and breathed against the glass.

Knock. Knock.

"Come on out," he said.

Knock. Knock.

I waited and breathed, waited and breathed. Sang a song to the spooky mirror girl and washed my hands. When Ella came home, I flushed the gaping toilet. I raced to Ella and we skipped outside, our hands grabbed tight like a hook and eye, singing, tired and weary and scattered everywhere.

NEWS PERSONALITY

Wayne Thomas

"Go ahead, caller. You're on the air."

"I'm on?"

"America's listening."

"Oh my god, I can't believe this is happening."

"You're actually inside the school, calling from your cellular phone? Do I understand that right?"

"Yes, sir."

"You're obviously a student. How old and what grade are you in?"

"I'm 15. I'm a sophomore."

"What's your name, honey?"

"Holly."

"Holly, can you tell me what you're seeing?"

"I'm in a closet. He started shooting, and I ran inside a janitor's closet. I see a mop and broom, a bunch of buckets, paper towels, some stuff in a bottle. I think it's ammonia. It's got a strong smell. I think I might pass out."

"Try and stay with us if you can, Holly."

"I'll try. I put the top back on the bottle."

"Good. Tell us what you saw before running into the closet."

"It was Dick."

"Dick?"

"He goes to school here. He's the one shooting. He mainly shoots them in the knees, but he shot some in the head."

"He shot student children in the head?"

"Just the ones he doesn't like. He doesn't like me, so I ran into the closet."

"We should point out that it's Holly naming the gunman and not this news corporation. We have yet to officially confirm who's responsible for this horrible massacre."

"Can I say hello to my boyfriend Mike? He skipped school today, so he's probably listening. Hi, Mike! I love you!"

"Holly, can we get you to briefly peep your head outside the closet and tell us what you see?"

"You really want me to do that?"

"Just for a second so we can get a clear idea of what it's like to be among this needless destruction."

"Okay. Hold on. I'll be right back."

SKIN

Ron Wallace

"This might sound strange," she says, "but I'm sort of worried about how we'll pay for the plastic surgery when I lose all that weight."

"Plastic surgery?" I say. We're walking along the beach at Mazomanie—inching along, really. At five-feet-two and two-hundred-fifty pounds—and with her ankle, foot, and knee problems—she can't move very fast, the August sun melting her buttery face. Discretely behind my sunglasses, I'm eyeing the thong bikinis, the fleshy tremolo of twenty-something centerfolds strutting their stuff around us.

"Well," she says, "I think about all that skin, empty of fat." She says she heard of a man who actually sold his excess skin to a medical supply company to help pay for the cosmetic treatments.

"No," I say. "That's ridiculous. It doesn't work that way. You might have a few wrinkles, but the skin shrinks as you lose weight. It's not like emptying a plastic grocery sack."

In all our months of talking about her weight—how she's going to lose it; how I like her fat; how thin is just a cultural affectation, a stinginess, a lack—we've never had this particular conversation. But then, she's always coming up with these oddball observations—how one of her friends at Weight Watchers was pregnant with twins and didn't know it until one day they just popped out; how she read of a man whose fat caught fire like tallow in a saucepan. And so, even thought it's crazy, I'm thinking about her skin splayed out like a huge hot air balloon, deflated, a thin loopy membrane of silk.

"Are you sure?" she says.

I roll my eyes and sigh as two tanned, oily haunches divided by a lone black thread pass us by. I try to imagine her in *that* body, trailing a billow of skin, the thin Mylar housing flapping, abandoned.

She takes my hand and I snap back, her sausagey fingers fueling my usual hunger.

"Hang onto your skin," I say, as we float slowly along toward a future that threatens to thin all around us. "Hang onto your skin."

And I hold onto her like a gondola holds onto a dirigible. And the turning world stares up at us, with envy and with wonder.

WORRY

Ron Wallace

She worried about people; he worried about things. And between them, that about covered it.

"What would you think of our daughter sleeping around?" she said.

"The porch steps are rotting," he replied. "Someone's going to fall through."

They were lying in bed together, talking. They had been lying in bed together talking these twenty-five years: first, about whether to have children—she wanted to (although there was Downs' Syndrome, leukemia, microcephalia, mumps); he didn't (the siding was warped; the roof was going fast)—and then, after their daughter was born, a healthy seven pounds eleven ounces ("She's not eating enough;" "The furnace is failing"), about family matters, mostly ("Her friends are hoodlums, her room is a disaster;" "The brakes are squealing, the water heater's rusting out").

Worry grew between them like a son, with his own small insistencies and then more pressing demands. They stroked and coddled him; they set a place for him at the table; they sent him to kindergarten, private school, and college. Because he failed at nearly everything and always returned home, they loved him. After all, he was their son.

"I've been reading her diary. She does drugs. She sleeps around."

"I just don't think I can fix them myself. Where will we find a carpenter?"

And so it went. Their daughter married her high school sweetheart, had a family, and started a health food store in a distant town. Although she recalled her childhood as fondly as anyone—how good her parents had been and how they worried for her, how old and infirm they must be growing, their house going to ruin—she rarely called or visited. She had worries of her own.

AFTER THE HEART

Mary Hussmann

Mrs. Cook leads me down the hallway and into a room chock full of board games and toys.

"Why don't you pick out a game to play with me? I'll be back in a few seconds," she says and shuts the door behind her.

I look around the room aimlessly. There's nothing here I want to play with, and especially not with *her*. I know why I'm here. I'm in "therapy." We're all in therapy, my mom and dad too. It's my seventh grade year except I've had what they call a "nervous breakdown" and I can't go to school so I stay home and have a tutor. I can't sleep because my head aches so badly all the time, and I always feel like throwing up. I'm afraid that if I let myself relax I'll really go crazy.

"Pick something out?" she chirps in that fakey voice I've learned to hate as she comes back in the room. I shrug. With her I'm even more evasive and withdrawn than at home.

"Okay, then, how about 'Operation'?" she says, putting the game between us on a table in the corner.

I know what she's up to; she wants to watch how I'm reacting to these stupid games, whether I get mad when I lose. I know she's trying to be nice, but I don't care. I want to beat her at her own game. She'll never figure me out. I've decided that I want to be an intellectual. Emotions are a sign of weakness, so I try not to have any.

I carefully maneuver the tweezers into the chest cavity. I'm after the heart. I accidentally touch the metal rim surrounding the opening. A buzzer sounds and a big red light in the patient's nose flashes. I lose my turn.

"It's all yours," I say with a smile, pushing the game back across the table. I'm not going to give her anything.

THE BOOK OF LIFE

Sarah Freligh

Begin with a yank, a slap, much crying. You have arrived. Your story can start.

Add secondary characters: A hero or two (a father, a mother). A villain or two (a father, a mother). Give them a conflict: She wants, he doesn't. She stays, he goes. She stays up nights drinking bad wine from a water glass, watching moths bang up against the light bulb over the front porch.

Just like your father, she says.

Let them live unhappily ever after.

Escalate conflict. You get older. You pity your heart, its solitary confinement, caged in the prison of your ribs. For a treat, you take your heart out on occasional Saturdays, wear it on your sleeve. Let life bump it around a little, scuff its innocent shine.

You fall in love.

Forget about happy. This is where conflict must rise to crisis. The fall is spectacular enough to break your heart, a comminuted fracture you're sure you won't survive. You stay up nights drinking bad wine from a water glass, watching CNN: A child born with wings and a tail, yellow eyes. The face of God rising over Fort Worth. Twin buildings bulldozed by airplanes on a late summer day

Your heart aches.

Suddenly you're old. You're leaning over a putt one day, two feet from a birdie on the eighteenth green, when your heart attacks you—a sneak assault, a commando raid—a volley of fire in your chest. Such a traitor, your heart, after all you've done for it. You drop to your knees and try to say *help*.

What comes out instead is *amen*.

ANOTHER THING

Sarah Freligh

That year the heat started after Memorial Day and didn't quit until Halloween. There was no rain to speak of. The corn shriveled up and slumped in the fields like old men who had run out of hope. A woman who claimed to be part Iroquois read the sky at night and told us all it was our last summer on earth.

My mother said the world couldn't end without a party. The first Saturday in August, my father strung Japanese lanterns between the trees in our back yard. My mother rolled her hair and put on stockings and a dress that showed her thighs when she danced. I walked around collecting dirty glasses on a cork-covered tray. The women pinched my cheek and told me how big I'd gotten, like they hadn't seen me for years.

The party got louder. The women left lipstick mouths on the rims of plastic glasses. The men rolled up their sleeves. I hid inside the willow tree behind the garage and ate the melting ice from two glasses of scotch. I heard a sound like the rustle of grass before a storm, but it was only my mother's dress as she moved closer to Mr. Cullen.

"Marie," he said, like there was something he had to say to her. There was the liquid clear sound of kissing and he didn't say another thing.

Late in the night, I watched father lead my mother onto the dance floor. She fit her body into his and smiled up at his eyes, her teeth bright against her dark lipstick. Their feet moved together in dangerous perfect time. When they turned, I could see her hand on his back, her nails like red holes in the white of his shirt.

That was our last summer after all.

WHY WOULD A WOMAN POUR BOILING WATER ON HER HEAD?

Jim Heynen

Why would a woman pour a pitcher of boiling water over her head while standing naked in a snow bank near a cabin in the north woods?

I was going to rinse my hair, she says, though we know there must be more to it.

See our woman with the flaming face inside the cabin now, rocking near the fire with a towel filled with ice pressed to her forehead. She was standing in snow when she burned her face, so she is trying to defrost her feet while chilling her face.

See a large stone fireplace with white-barked birch and sweet-fragranced cedar burning in a calm flame.

See a moose head from the 1920s pondering the scene from the log walls.

See old encyclopedias, magazines from the 40s, a piano with withered ivory.

See open rafters and a balcony with dark sleeping quarters overhead.

The room divides between moonlight and fire light, between pleasure and pain, between fire and ice.

Feel her burning misery, but hear her say, It is the mystery of the incongruous, as if this were enough to accept the skin on the bridge of her nose skimming loose like the film on stale cream at the touch of her finger. It is the mystery of the incongruous, she repeats, and offers a smile to all who will listen. I feel as if I have sinned, she says, and that I am being punished. But my sin, my sin, it was so ordinary.

THE WAX APPLE

Michael Waters

Grandmother never spoke numbers: years, family. Her losses were formal, tattooed near the wrist, like blue lace.

After the war, she spent hours polishing the wax apple, dusting the green skin to glare. On the windowsill, the apple blazed like a skull.

Often, blinding a row of scrub oak, the apple reflected a bright plot of sunlight. Then Grandmother would witness the holocaust from each distant corner of the room.

She would circle faster and faster, until the apple seemed to spin, the room dissolve, until she stood, again, among apples—not far from her home in that lost country.

JCB

Michael Waters

On the lawn, the grape arbor drags its carcass toward the moon. It looks like the last woolly mammoth, large and shaggy, hauling its shoulderful of sparrows toward extinction. An unmistakable odor of sadness surrounds it, the odor of rotting vines, the rich scent of mouse dung and shriveled grapes.

Once a family played croquet on this lawn. The son had an artificial arm that gleamed in the sunlight. Whenever he lost, his metal hand grasped the winner's in a technological advance.

Soon their lawn will be gone. The Appalachian Highway has already touched the neighbor's meadow with its leper's fingers. The house will be trucked to another hill, the grape arbor burned and carted away.

This morning I found a mallet in the garage. On the curved head was carved: "My mallet, 1944, JCB." I imagine the one-armed boy, missing the war, propping the shaft between his knees one afternoon. Using his knife, he wanted to claim something solid, forever, for his own.

THE DEPARTMENT STORY BEAR

David Kress

At night, late, after Sam the guard has made his last round and has gone off to grab thirty minutes of illegal and undeserved sleep, the Department Story Bear comes to life and roams the empty aisles. He's in sporting goods, thwacking arrows into the ceiling in a daffodil pattern. Rambling the men's shoe section, he mixes up the display case so that a white buck is paired with a penny loafer, a wingtip with a rubber, a sneaker with a cowboy boot, a—

With absolutely no reserve, he peeks up under the skirts of the mannequins in the women's clothing department. He finds comfort and pleasure in their shared asexuality. He walks down the up escalator and flushes a urinal over and over until it overflows onto the floor of the men's room on two. As Sam snaps awake, the Department Story Bear hurries back to its shelf in toys and dies again. Its last thought, before returning to infinity, is, "A pity. Small appliances..."

REVENGE

Karen Blomain

Stale summer evening hits me as I leave Portman Hall. It's rained. Damp blacktop gives off vapors, dense and tropical. Dry rectangles where students have reclaimed their cars score the lot. Last out of the building, I've ordered my office life after lingering students. I'm mining my handbag for keys before I hear the metallic syllable of the security lock behind me.

Across the shimmering, far back beyond my Subaru, I notice one other car just as I feel him behind me. As he pulls me backwards against the brick wall, my bag catches on the ashtray beside the door. The butt studded tureen of sand teeters. Contents of both scatter—the stuff of my life—glasses, mascara, money, credit cards, everything I hold close—mixes with the ashy sand and half smoked cigarettes.

Before I can respond, he says, "Remember me?" His even breath, warm and fetid as July air, the voice unfamiliar. "No," I squeak, hoping he'll speak again. I try to turn, but he yanks me roughly forward. He's just out of view behind my left shoulder.

"I don't want to frighten you, Lydia, but you shouldn't be here so late at night alone."

In a register I'd never used before, I blurt an unintelligible "wheep."

"Be more careful," his voice playful, "You don't know what nasty surprise is waiting around the corner." Suddenly, he's jerks to the ground, an involuntarily genuflection. As I whip my head around to see him, his right hand shoots up in front of me. The sand stings my face; pain searing my eyes. My tongue moves the grit against my teeth.

When I can rub my eyes and look, he's gone.

MAY 13, 1982

Karen Blomain

Her father in his lucky tie, and her mother in a column of green, herself in front, connected to them by the casual crisscross of their arms?

All their days collapsed into one.

True: they had lived on Gordon Street in that brick rowhouse. From the bed in her parents' room she watched her father wrap his fragile belongings in squares of gray flannel, rags torn from old pajamas. Silver maples pods helicoptered onto the porch roof. The curtains luffed at the open window.

Bittersweet, the armful of mock oranges on the breakfast table. They ate together when he was not traveling.

In the moments of spooning and chewing and swallowing, of moving their arms and faces, the gestures of ordinary life the photo doesn't show, her father was already leaving them and her mother's heart winding down. Beneath their clothing, their bodies readied for what could not be changed.

On the porch her mother turned back. "A picture," she said, bright lipstick around her mouth, "of the last time you'll be leaving us." She held the camera out toward a passing workman, saying "Please," then putting her hand to her throat. The man took the camera and waved his arm to frame them by the steps.

"A promise," her father said, "The last time." They had agreed next time he would stay.

The obscene, the holy photograph. Solid in their bodies, anchored by each other's arms against the gusts that spun her skirt and swirled the seeds along her bare calves, they stood behind her looking happy.

Her father left.

Her mother died.

But what of that unlucky child, center of the picture, looking as if she were not looking? If she had been, would she have known that her world was ending?

MOMMA'S BOY

Melissa Fraterrigo

Joseph flung open the back door of the two-bedroom rental home and sprinted into the bathroom while Carlotta paid bills at the table, the help-wanted ads in a stack at her left, breakfast dishes still soaking in the sink. "Joey? What do you have?"

She shut the door. The fan on top of the refrigerator blew a hot gust on her face. Yesterday it was a kitten. Three days ago he brought home a gray rabbit from a girl two blocks over. If they lived closer to her brothers, Carlotta wouldn't worry about Joey, but Detroit was a six-hour ride by train and with her salary at Sunshine Dental, they wouldn't be making any trips until Christmas. "Joseph Michael Vespi, I'm talking to you."

He unlocked the door and crept into the kitchen. Mud speckled his glasses; his dark bangs slumped against his forehead. Joseph held out his cupped palms and inside was a green and yellow-shelled thing. "It's a turtle, mom. He was sitting near the train tracks. I saved him."

"Joey." Tugging on his wrist, she led him outside. Squinting into the light, Carlotta placed the turtle on the sidewalk; it remained motionless. "Now hit him. You're a boy." Joey trembled. "No crying, hit him." He bent down and tapped its shell with two fingers. Snot dribbled from the end of his nose. Carlotta drew her hand into a fist and pounded its shell. "You're a boy. A boy." She smacked it again and something popped and the turtle flattened. Suddenly her breath snapped and jerked out of her lungs; she was tossed backwards, the pavement burning her skin. Joey stood on top of her, his shoes making two muddy blobs on her blouse. She peered up at him. "Good," she said. "That's good."

NICARAGUA

Kirk Nesset

What you leave out, describing it all, is the girl. How pretty she was—petite, exquisitely cheek-boned, Norwegian. The way she bumped your shoulder with hers in the dark as you walked toward the lake. A walk, you thought, was the appropriate move. You don't say to nice girls in hotels, even down there, in Spanish less polished than hers, Want to adjourn to my room? The fact is the lake after dark is not safe. You didn't know. Or didn't know what you knew.

What you leave out is everything. The lovely near-perfect Spanish with its Scandinavian lilt. The world dropping parcel by parcel away in the pastel candlelit bar. Her delicate chin, cheeks sprinkled with freckles. The story you tell is bare action, assailants gliding from shadows, surreal. Why dwell on what happened after? She came to your room and you sat in shock, bed to bed, talking. Inert you remained, sans passport, sans bank checks, plastic and cash, no coins even to get a cab to the cop station. Why regret what you might have done and did not? Like lay down beside her, attempt the comfort that nearness might bring?

What you leave out is why you went to Nicaragua at all. You don't really know. All you know—later—is that you bottomed out there in intricate ways. Robbery was merely the ostensible way, the part that most palpably grates.

The *calle*, the city, the very country grows progressively nasty, more filthy, desperate, each time you tell it. The number of assailants increase. They're men now, not boys, each armed with a knife. In truth you saw only one blade. The girl didn't see any.

LADYBUG INN

Kirk Nesset

Four Dirt Devil bags of bugs in three weeks. They might fill four more. War, this was. Her windows had been too long defiled, her hilltop sweep of Christmas card meadow persistently sullied. This was their house. They'd dreamed the thing into form and lo, it arose: foundation, frame, massy creek boulder chimney, the endless glass. They married—third time for her—and moved in. Then the ladybugs came. They came and came and kept coming. Henry turned funny.

She steadied the ladder, aluminum feet aligned with hers on the rug. Henry swayed, all belly, above. He was gaping out at the snow now, Dirt Devil raging.

Henry, she yelled. She smacked the ladder with the heel of her hand. Then reached and unplugged the cord.

Stunned he stood in the ladybug stink, clutching the vacuum and gray vacuum tube. He looked at her finally. He stared from some unknown dimension, where space and time and the gas bill dissolved and bug shit on windows seemed petty. She knew then what she'd known all along, that the house indeed was a dream, as they were; that, though the cat-scan didn't happen till Wednesday, the machine would cry Tumor, tumor; there'd be the lightning decline and post-blizzard funeral, the horrendous contest in court: Martha Clapsaddle versus the bloodthirsty kids.

Henry, she said. He grunted; he managed the penultimate rung. He raised the vacuum, addressing a red splash of bugs. Saying: Why ain't it working.

She looked at him. Sighed. And plugged it back in.

Sometimes it seemed they were winning. Down they'd go, hundreds, the bastards, in the stabbing December sun. And down they went now. *Little fuckers!* This wasn't Ladybug Inn, nor would it be ever. The tick of the ladybug-suck in the roar still afforded her pleasure.

SOMETIMES WE TELL A STORY WITHOUT SAYING A WORD

Gail Galloway Adams

Breakfast:

Monday: Cheerios and banana, hazelnut coffee. Only read the Sports.

Tuesday: The same.

Wednesday: Stale strawberry pop tart and half an apple; read circular from Papa John's Pizza: Two two two for the price of one.

Thursday: More of this.

Friday: Nothing and nothing and nothing but two cups of coffee and no cream. Napkins pile up on the floor.

Saturday: Bed linens, sham covers gray and smelling of stale self; rain outside and in.

Sunday: Remember a day of french toast with hot honey and confectionary's sugar in drifts and bacon's sizzle and laughter and nesting in the comforter with all the children around. On the outside the two bigger boys embarrassed to be called into hugs with the family, but doing it all the same because that's what a family does when things were too bad or too sad; all the little ones scooched up tight and warm in one loving lump... Pull down in the pillows, more redolent now, thinking: hunger and hunger and hunger.

THE DARK SIDE OF THE MOON

Mark Budman

When I was six, I waded into the Black Sea until the water reached my cute belly button. I asked my father, "What's on other side?"

"Bulgaria," he said. That sounded mealy, like an arid bagel.

"And after that?"

"Western Europe."

I knew what a Western was—a movie where they ride horses and fight Indians.

"And after that?"

"The Atlantic ocean."

"And behind the ocean?"

"America."

I knew Americans wore top hats, smoked cigars, exploited workers and wanted to bomb everybody, especially my Motherland. But I didn't know they were that far.

"What is closer, America or the moon?"

"Spanking," my dad said with his usual half-smile. "That's the closest thing to you." He thought for a second and added, "Violence determines conciseness."

I didn't know he was making a Russian language pun on the Marxist maxim "Environment determines conciseness."

Many years later, I stood at the New Jersey shore and watched clouds eat the pale moon by the Eastern horizon. The cell phone rang.

"It's better be good," I said.

"It's done, boss," was the reply.

I hung up and stuck my cigar back into my mouth. If you blow the whistle in my company, you won't last long.

A FOREIGN X

Dimitri Anastasopoulos

In mornings I await coffee arriving quick on the end of first cigarette, cup. Waitress lean over, red chili sarong too big for slight woman loose open with sash just dangle over coffee cup, cup. Very polite, even in Foreign X, her eyes trained on my chest, cup. Almost beautiful, for Foreign X, and very slight so rare, cup-d-cup.

"Is toast of need?" waitress ask, and then with too polite obligated punctual, "ca."

XX manners not attractive when foreign uttered, cup. This I not speak to her in loudness, cup.

"Yes, cup," I say to her.

"And marmalade, ca?" she ask.

"Cup-d-cup."

I cannot continue this puppet show every morning, cup. Even if café is closest to my home humble, puppet life is not for me, cup. Must find new café, cup, I think to myself. Must not let Foreign X butcher of XX tradition invade for worse my well-being, cup. Must not wait for café owner to fire waitress, cup. As promised, cup. Two weeks now and still waiting…

At new café extra kilometer from home I take seat and observe surroundings fresh, cup. Indeed, cup-d-cp. XX waitress, cup. Subtle and shy, she come with dainty foot and bow to my chest deference, cup. Appreciation-filled is descriptive of my mental state, cup. XX woman disappoints only in beauty, though even defects noted appeal stronger to me than Foreign X, cup. A natural law, cup.

"Good morning cup." I offer attentions.

She regard my chest deference, and with voice polish she say, "Is coffee of need, ca?"

I hear all difference, cup.

DAPPLED MARIA

Jamey Gallagher

Dappled Maria with her swollen womb has come again. Left again. Come again, again. She buys three emaciated weenies on three crusted rolls. She buys a Super Slurpie and three packs of Virginia Slims. She buys a small, overpriced round of oatmeal. A packaged brownie hard as stone. She takes five books of matches and smiles gap-toothed.

Is any of this my fault?

She has a dynamic skin condition. I've watched her smoke under the stunted pine tree by the parking lot, opening a carton of coffee milk, picking at scabs on her legs. When she comes out of the shadows her skin retains the markings. She's like a panther or a chameleon -- one of those changelings. But what good could her ability do her?

She doesn't smell healthy. I have worked here for nine months, and she's been pregnant that whole time. I have not said a word to her.

She buys packages of super-sized tampons. Chiclets. Twinkies. Minute Maid Lemonade cans. Teriyaki beef jerky. I know she's pregnant because I've watched her breasts growing, swelling with sweet milk. Also, she glows. She buys small, imperfect produce.

Is there anything I can do to help her?

Dappled Maria lives in the apartments across the street. She has a mother, children. She works out of a small, cluttered room, stuffing envelopes. She's like Penelope, waiting for a husband to return, rejecting all suitors. She buys frozen pizzas, frozen burritos, frozen waffles, ice cream sandwiches. She waddles across the road, one bag under each arm.

Someday twins will burst out of her. They'll have the same skin condition. They'll be like a new race of man. I'll watch them with interest.

I CARRY A HAMMER IN MY POCKET FOR OCCASIONS SUCH AS THESE

Anthony Tognazzini

A guy I didn't like approached me on the street. He was wearing a backwards baseball cap and cream colored jeans. He might have said Hey man howzitgoing? He might have said Where you headin' or You aren't going to believe what happened to me today. I cast him a glance that read rapacious hatred.

He said, "You know why you don't like me, man?"

I said, "Lay it on me."

He said, "The reason you don't like me is because you don't like yourself."

I said, "Is that so?"

He said, "Yeah, perhaps a little sensitivity on your part."

I said, "You think?"

He said, "Yeah, we project onto others our deepest fears and self-loathing."

"You may be right," I said, considering.

We walked awhile together on the street in silence, busses rushing past us. I thought about it. He was right. I knew he was right. After a time the guy asked if he could borrow some money from me. "No problem," I said, and reached in my pocket for the hammer.

A GIRL

Peter H. Conners

A girl was a bicycle and she didn't like her paint. She liked her wheels but hated her reflectors. Her rims were slightly bent. This caused her great suffering. She stood on the curb of an endless bicycle parade, not a race, and each one glided past truer, smoother, and bolted tighter than she. Lamenting her poor drooping chain she beckoned a friend, *be a baseball card. Ride in my spokes. Chatter as we go and surely they will not hear the squeaking of my joints.* But the friend turned into a kite and flew away. *You will be my streamers!* A man with a package and coattails just long enough to latch onto came close enough: *Be my streamers,* she demanded. *You will flutter in colors of the rainbow as I roll by and one day perhaps they will forgive the dullness of my hue.* But the man jumped into the package, sealed and mailed himself back home. *Mother,* she wept tilting onto her kickstand, *Father,* she moaned crashing to the grass, *how could you saddle me with such a tattered seat, poor steering and undependable brakes? Surely you will become the orange flags trailing over my head pulling their eyes upward and away from the horrible flatness of my tires, this endless slow leak.* But her parents were a worm and a bird: one ate the other and gracefully alighted on a nearby tree branch, neatly preening. The girl rocked and put herself right, sadly rolling off down the street. All through the neighborhood one could hear the squeaking of her wheels, but grease would take years to find its way.

KATE AND CHAS GOT MARRIED

Julie Stotz-Ghosh

I had to watch the goldfish throughout dinner, in bowls, on glass. A strange centerpiece. The water stirred when we rapped our silverware on the table. Kate and Chas kissed. The sights and sounds made me nauseous, although, singly, I might have thought each one a beautiful thing.

I danced with one of the groomsmen, my brother, my uncle, my cousin, my father, the groom (for a dollar), the groom's adolescent brother, some guy who crashed the party, some guy who kept responding to conversation by saying "Yeah, Oooh-kay, yeah, thaaat's nice," and the limo driver, "from Kenya."

I saved the goldfish out of pity. I didn't know whether to put them in the sun or what to feed them. They ate bread crumbs before I got them the real stuff, fortified fish flakes. I figured they would die, so I didn't give them names.

Between bites of wedding cake, people speculated about how long Kate and Chas would stay together. Some gave the couple a year.

Two days after the wedding, I named my fish Bubbles and Goldy. I tried to keep it simple, generic, noncommittal. But a name is a name. The first step toward intimacy. This means they're going to die for sure. I've already pictured the way they'll look, belly-up. I hope, at least, that they'll go together, and soon. I imagine my cool reaction, relief, the welling up and sinking down inside my body the day this happens.

When my goldfish swim, they make funny faces. Their mouths say, "Dope, Dope, Dope," which gives me the impression that they're not too smart. They seem responsive to music. They move more, in wider circles. Maybe it's something to do with sound waves. Cello concertos have the greatest effect.

The first time I met Chas, I drove with Kate in her BMW to pick him up from work. To a hayfield, in the back country, in the dark, late July. I sneezed the whole way to the barn. We saw an owl on the branch of a tree. The moon made shadows on road. We followed behind his tractor—his hazard lights on, our hazard lights on, blinking for miles.

POST SCRIPT

Bret Lott

It seemed he would never get the words, never find the right ones for the story. Things happened around him: his children came in with Lego problems, his friends called, his mother grew old, his father up and died on him, his children left the house for hours on end with the car, then came back, years later, with other children, children of their own. And still his wife called to him with chores, chores that seemed only more clutter: bring the garbage to the garage, mow the lawn, oil this door, pack these boxes, sign here on this line and drive the truck four states west, then help me with the corn, keep the silk inside the sink.

All this each afternoon, while still he sat with these words swirling about him in absurd order, words lined up like drunken soldiers, like harlots with painted lips slurring just as drunkenly as those soldiers he'd thought up. But even that idea of words like harlots and soldiers lined up before him began to stink of a lie—how could words line up like drunken soldiers and harlots?—this entire endeavor an absurdity in itself, while around him now his mother died and still more children paraded through the house and his own children, the children who had had those Lego problems only this morning, gave up to him their cares, came into his room where he tried to work and told him of mortgages and insurance rates and tuition costs, all cares of a world he wanted out of in order to get these words right, get these lost and swirling words in line before him, in some sort of order, so that they might bow to him, he imagined, might surrender to him, perhaps, a moon over a midnight lake, its surface flat and black and clean, so smooth that now there came a second moon just beneath the first, a moon that descended into its own black sky, this lake, the higher its sister moon rose over this lake of words he wanted smoothed for him.

That was what he wanted: that moon. Both of them. Maybe even that black sky thrown in for good measure.

But nothing came to him. No moons, no midnight lakes. Eventually, too, his wife stopped calling to him in the afternoon, oiled doors, kept the silk inside the sink, kissed the children goodbye, until finally he looked up one night, saw outside his window a sky gone the perfect black of a midnight sky, a perfect moon rising just like a moon.

All by itself, no help from him at all.

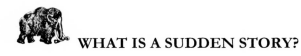 **WHAT IS A SUDDEN STORY?**

Wherein various authors bravely attempt to describe what may be indescribable.

Bret Lott, author of POST SCRIPT

I really don't know what the heck it is, save for the fact it is almost always—and I mean this sincerely, without any sense of hyperbole whatsoever—a moment stripped of everything to reveal truly, deeply, a matter of life and death.

Nicholas DiChario, author of SWEATERS

Think of a fine piece of dark chocolate, solid and succulent. When you take it in, the taste snaps in your mouth. For one brief moment, you crave nothing but the visceral joy it delivers. It has done more than nourish and sustain, it has transcended the mundane. It is narcotically decadent. It happens so suddenly, so unexpectedly, you want more.

Richard Pearse, author of CAT CUSTODY

Instead of hyper-hyphenizing ("short-short-short-story" as in "off-off-off-Broadway"), let's think of this microsmic form as living, oblivious of tariffs, on the borders of fiction and poetry, and not far from the shores of drama. Verbal pyrotechnics are as available to it as plotting. It can be comic, tragic, or lyrical in an instant. But it's not a parasite: this mighty mite of a form returns to its larger, often more preoccupied, hosts a variety of quick-change possibilities and techniques. Long may it shorten!

Angus Woodward, author of ONE THING YOU MUST
       NEVER DO

POW it's in front of you and you go through it and it ends and you suddenly stop and it's over and BOOM it resonates, which is the wrong word because we're not talking about a gong here. We're talking about a rifle shot.

Paola Corso, author of THE RIVER INSIDE HER

If writing fiction is the equivalent of being confined in a box, then the novelist's box is big enough for her to take a long walk. The short story writer can stand and stretch comfortably in his box, but the sudden story writer or prose poet's box has just enough air to breathe; the difference between the two is how labored the breaths.

Clint McCown, author of FINGERLINGS

An unwieldy meteor blisters through the atmosphere, burning itself down toward a smaller, more shapely core. No larger than a pebble, it strikes the surface of a lake, and waves radiate outward toward every shore. Witnesses drive straight home to tell their neighbors.

Mark Budman, author of THE DARK SIDE OF THE MOON

Paraphrasing an unknown animal rights violator who said that there is more than one way to skin a cat, there is more than one way to define flash or sudden fiction. In my definition, flash is the most concentrated, intense and poetic sub-genre of fiction. A good flash, replete with a cohesive plot, rich language and enticing imagery, is perhaps the hardest type of fiction to write. A good flash is so condensed that it borderlines poetry. A good flash engages your mind not only for the short duration of its read, but for a long time after.

Brent Spencer, author of CLASS REPORT and DOWN IN
    THE JUNGLE ROOM

I love the quick in-and-out of the short-short form, the literary equivalent of the smash-and-grab robbery.

Maurice Kilwein Guevara, author of FAST FORWARD and GRIMM THE JANITOR

A sudden story: Waking up one fine Sunday morning in September with a case of Bell's palsy, the left side of your face paralyzed, not sure whether you're laughing at the mirror or frightened to death, not sure whether it will last a few weeks or forever.

Jennifer Cande, author of BAD DOG

I think what's interesting about shorts is that they are as fast paced as our own lives now seem. The sentences, phrases, and words must multi-task in order to be efficient and successful. They are real Type-A stories! And then, of course, if you take this metaphor to its logical end, it's possible to begin to consider the blast of insight or irony of the short's last lines, as the metaphorical heart attacks, or nervous breakdowns of the structure of the piece.

Peter Markus, author of GIRL, GIRL IS A RIVER, and WHAT WE DO WITH THE FISH AFTER WE GUT THE FISH

The short-short/sudden story isn't afraid to be strange, or absurd, or silly, or poetic. It can tell a straight-forward story if straight-forward is what it sets out to tell. Or it cannot. If it would rather leap, or take the crooked path around convention, then leap or run crooked it will go. It takes pride in making its own path. It makes and lives by its own set of rules. It is a short-short fiction, it is a poem, it is the first and last and only page of a single-paged novel. In short, at the heart of it: it is the core of the tree. In a short-short, even a comma makes a difference. Even the space between words makes a sound.

William Heyen, author of ERATO: THE POET AT SIXTY and EXPERIENCE

A sudden story is a roll-top desk on a surfboard. No, it's not. It's a shovel whose handle is a stick of dynamite, blade a Claymore mine. No, it's not. It's an ecosystem. Yes, it is. How's the air, water, soil in there? Look at the size of all those dragonflies on all those lily pads! Look at the clouds reflected in the eyes of all those fish and turtles rising to surface!

Josh Russell, author of BLACK CAT and "WINTER ON
    FIFTH AVENUE, NEW YORK"

Perhaps this quote from Primo Levi's Periodic Table can somehow be my answer: "Distillation is beautiful."

Denise Duhamel, author of READING GROUP
    DISCUSSION GUIDE

Prose poetry and flash fiction are kissing cousins. They are kissing on Jerry Springer, knowing they're cousins, and screaming "So what?" as the audience hisses. They're kissing on One Life to Live, unaware one's aunt is the other's mother. A prose poem suffers from amnesia, and when her friends tell her about her past, nothing they describe produces in her even a flicker. In a flash, she thinks: they are wrong—something tells me I was once a short short. Flash fiction looks into the mirror and sees a prose poem. A prose poem parts his hair on the left instead of the middle, and his barber tells him he's flash fiction. A prose poem walks into a bar, and the bartender says, "What'll you have? The usual paragraph?" A flash fiction walks into the doctor's office and the doctor says, "How's that stanza feeling?" There may be a difference between flash fiction and prose poems, but I believe the researchers still haven't found the genes that differentiate them.

Dimitri Anastasopoulos, author of A FOREIGN X

A sudden story is a surly state, spontaneous and spasmodic: a kick from a horse.

Karen Blomain, author of REVENGE and MAY 13, 1982

You go into Karawana's Weiners in Carbondale and take the last booth. Someone brings you coffee in a thick nicotine colored mug. A paper on the table, folded twice squints and you catch a few words. It's a letter. Five years ago, Marlene wanted Helene to know that Frederick had lost his leg. The money was safe, but they'd never see the baby again or the earrings. She was sorry and signed it love. When you look up, the old fellow in the cap and suspenders at the next booth is watching you.

Whatever was there grows. You smell that grease and flinch from his gaze almost every day. Marlene? Helene? You jolt to a stop. Your eyes float to the shoes of every Frederick you meet. You make out the earrings-one day filigree, the next cloisonné-and count the bills you and Marlene stole from the box Frederick had nailed far back at the bottom of a kitchen shelf. The next day, it's clearer. The guy with the cap must be Frederick and the leg thing was a ruse. Maybe. Did Helene ever get the letter? Where's the baby now?

Michael A. Arnzen, author of IN THE MIDDLE

A sudden story is like an active verb: it's an efficiency narrative. A jump cut into another world. An ice cube of plot whose theme thaws with time. "Flash" fiction uses a photographer's metaphor —a flashbulb bursting to capture a momentary "snapshot" of life. But sudden fiction is faster than the speed of light. There is no photographer framing the scene and squeezing the bulb; even before you begin a sudden story, you're already immersed in it.

Kirk Nesset, author of NICARAGUA and LADYBUG INN

If the short story constitutes, as William Trevor notes, the "art of the glimpse," then the sudden story constitutes the art of the post-glimpse, the tease-glimpse, the glimpse that almost was not. Sudden stories commence en ultima res, burning toward their ultimate ends; they leave faint hints in the ash about middles, about the way things begin.

Corey Mesler, author of HARMON'S DILEMMA

What is it about flash fiction, what draws the writer to it? What draws the reader? Ideally, what happens in microfiction is a small explosion, a detonation remarkable for its brilliance as much as its unexpectedness. Is this different from the longer story? Is there plot, character development, rising action, etc.? It is different. Sometimes. And sometimes, hopeful listeners, all these things cohere and you have a small story carrying a big load, doing what its big brothers do, but compactly, allusively, circumspectly, and then, at the end, if all is well, a little brain flare.

Lee Martin, author of SO YOU THINK YOU'RE SMART

I've often used the sudden story in my fiction writing classes because its concentrated form magnifies so many aspects of craft: a quick start in the midst of instability, the light-handed shading of crucial exposition, a rapidly building tension, a turn that brings out some additional and significant aspect of character or situation, a graceful end that resonates with more truth than we ever thought we had the right to expect. Write a sudden story and you "suddenly" (oh, God of Puns, please forgive me) feel the way a story moves: a bobsled frantically shoved away from the starting gate, riders hopping aboard and ducking their heads as the sled gathers speed, tips and angles as it slings through a turn. A sudden story does once what a longer story can do as many times as its forward motion can sustain. In a sudden story, once is enough. Once is all you have.

Sherrie Flick, author of BACK

It's like one of those instant towels you can buy at the Dollar Store. There it is, this entire "real" towel condensed down to a little hard puck of a thing sitting in a heap right by the checkout. You don't trust it, think it's a scam, but then when you get home, you add water, and bam, you have a wash cloth sporting a puppy in a basket or a lion brushing his teeth.

Wendy Ring, author of ROCKET SCIENCE

Sudden stories are the fiction equivalent of freeze dried food with vacuum-packed characters and compressed action rendered in compact language ... only sudden stories are way more satisfying than powdered cheddar cheese.

Keith Carter, author of BOUNCING

A sudden story is the complete and absolute distillation of a story into its purest form, the boiling off of all extraneous and unnecessary language, resulting in fiction so concentrated and spare that each word has the thickness of a bouillon cube.

Lori Ann Stephens, author of HORSE HEAVY

The jewel of the sudden story is the gap. A lot of words are missing, not because they're extraneous, but because their absence speaks the unspeakable. The writer of the sudden story has to weigh the efficacy of each word. Knowing what to include—often the details—and knowing what not to include—often everything but the details—that's not a gift. It's a practice that involves trusting the written word more than yourself.

Christina Milletti, author of KASPAR SOUP

Write the bare bones, reveal the vertebrae, the underpinnings, that make a story stand up straight, or when crooked, why it bends, humpbacked, like an old man in search of his slippers. Flash fiction is hard, compact. Spare and white. Yet make the incision into bone, and you expose nerves, a quiet dialogue between each vertebra and another, which, in their brief and sudden conversations, often smart. Or cause sharp pain.

Susannah Breslin, author of EULOGY (FOR MY FATHER)

A sudden story is "Jesus wept" in long form.

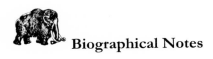 **Biographical Notes**

Gail Galloway Adams is an Associate Professor of English at West Virginia University. She is the author of *The Purchase of Order,* and has published stories in *Chattahoochee Review, Kestrel, North American Review,* and numerous other journals.

Dimitri Anastasopoulos is a Visiting Assistant Professor of English at the University of Rochester. His first novel, *A Larger Sense of Harvey,* was published in 2001 by MAMMOTH books.

Nin Andrews is the author of several books including *The Book of Orgasms,* and *Why They Grow Wings.* She has published in numerous literary reviews and anthologies including *Best American Poetry* (1997 and 2001), *The Best of the Prose Poem, The Virginia Quarterly, The Paris Review* and *Ploughshares.*

Jane Armstrong's work has appeared in *Newsweek, The North American Review, Beloit Fiction Journal, New Orleans Review* and elsewhere. She teaches at Northern Arizona University and is an editor at Universities West Press and *Mississippi Review.*

Michael A. Arnzen teaches writing and popular fiction at Seton Hill University. His latest books are the poetry collections *Gorelets: Unpleasant Poetry* and *Freakcidents: A Surrealist Sideshow.* Arnzen won the Bram Stoker Award for his first horror novel, *Grave Markings,* in 1995. He resides online at gorelets.com.

Melissa Gurley Bancks is currently the managing editor for *River Styx* and has works forthcoming or appearing in *Boulevard, Sou'wester, The Big Muddy, The U. S. Latino Review, The Cape Rock,* and elsewhere. Her collection of poems, *On the Shoulders of Sparrows,* was awarded second place in the National Society of Arts and Letters St. Louis Chapter Contest.

Aimee Bender is the author of two books: a collection of stories, *The Girl in the Flammable Skirt,* and a novel, *An Invisible Sign of My Own.* She lives in Los Angeles.

Karen Blomain is a poet, essayist, and fiction writer. Her first novel, *A Trick of Light,* was published by Toby Press: London, 2001. Barwood Films has acquired the screen rights. Blomain teaches in the Professional Writing Program at Kutztown University of Pennsylvania.

David Booth currently teaches creative writing at the University of San Francisco. His fiction has appeared in *The Missouri Review* and *Quick Fiction;* his poetry, in *Transfer* and *Fourteen Hills.* His novel, *The Itinerants,* is forthcoming.

Tom Bradley is a novelist exiled in Nagasaki. Various of his five published novels have been nominated for the Editor's Book Award, the New York University Bobst Prize, and the AWP Award. Excerpts and reviews, links to Tom's online publications (*Exquisite Corpse, Salon, McSweeney's,* etc.), plus recorded readings, are posted at tombradley.org.

Susannah Breslin is a Los Angeles-based creator of fiction, essays, photos, and comix. Her work can be found in FC2's *Chick Lit 2* postfeminist fiction anthology, *Fantagraphics' Dirty Stories* Volume 3, and in various other venues.

Nickole Brown is a poet and fiction writer currently attending the MFA Program for Creative Writing at Vermont College. She graduated summa cum laude from University of Louisville and studied English Literature at Oxford University as an English Speaking Union Scholar. She works at Sarabande Books.

Mark Budman has been published in *Mississippi Review, Virginia Quarterly, Happy, Web Del Sol, Parting Gifts,* and elsewhere. *Exquisite Corpse* nominated him for the XXVI Pushcart Prize. He is the publisher of *Vestal Review.*

Jotham Burrello is a Chicago-based writer and video producer. He teaches in the fiction writing department at Columbia College Chicago. His work has appeared in various journals.

Jennifer Cande has completed a BFA in Writing, Literature and Publishing at Emerson College in Boston. She is a founding co-editor of *Quick Fiction*, a publication of stories under 500 words. Her work has appeared in *Paragraph* magazine.

Keith Loren Carter is currently enrolled in the MFA Program in Creative Writing at Emerson. He is learning, by trial and error, how to write a novel, which will not only have to succeed on its own, but also enjoy the added burden of serving as his thesis project.

Jose Chaves writes poetry, short-shorts and creative nonfiction. His work has appeared in *The Atlanta Review, The Northwest Review* and *Rattle.* He has also published a book of translations of the Latin American short-short entitled, *The Book of Brevity.*

Rita Ciresi is the author of two story collections—*Mother Rocket* and *Sometimes I Dream in Italian*—and three novels—*Blue Italian, Pink Slip,* and *Remind Me Again Why I Married You.* She lives with her husband and daughter in Wesley Chapel, Florida.

Antonia Clark writes short fiction and poetry. She works as a medical writer, researching medical literature and developing the content of medical diagnostic software tools. She lives in Burlington, Vermont.

Judith Ortiz Cofer is the author of several books in various genres. Her work has appeared in *Georgia Review, Kenyon Review, the Southern Review,* and has been anthologized in *The Best American Essays, The Norton Book of Women's Lives, The Pushcart Prize,* and the *O. Henry Prize Stories.* A native of Puerto Rico, she now resides in Georgia where she is the Franklin Professor of English and Creative Writing at the University of Georgia.

Peter H. Conners lives in Rochester, NY. His fiction and poetry appear regularly in literary journals, and his two completed novels are under representation by the Linda Roghaar Literary Agency. He is founding co-editor of *Double Room: A Journal of Prose Poetry & Flash Fiction* on Web Del Sol. He maintains the website: www.peterconners.com.

Paola Corso, recipient of the 2000 Sherwood Anderson Fiction Prize, has been published in numerous literary journals and anthologies. Her poetry chapbook, *A Proper Burial,* is forthcoming from Pudding House Publications. A Pittsburgh area native, she currently teaches fiction at Fordham University in New York City.

Chauna Craig has published fiction in *Prairie Schooner, CALYX, Green Mountains Review, South Dakota Review, Ascent, Passages North, Quarterly West,* and elsewhere. A former Bread Loaf wait-scholar and graduate of Arizona State and the University of Nebraska, she teaches creative writing at Indiana University of Pennsylvania.

Born in Wales, **Laurence Davies** now lives in Vermont. His short and very short fiction has appeared in *Story Quarterly* and *New England Review.* Currently he is finishing a novel: *The Cup of the Dead.*

Todd Davis is associate professor of English at Goshen College, where he teaches creative writing, film, and American literature. His poems have appeared in numerous literary reviews, including *The North American Review, Yankee, Image, Many Mountains Moving, The Nebraska Review,* and many others. His first book of poetry, *Ripe,* was published by Bottom Dog Press in 2002.

Nicholas DiChario's short fiction has appeared in many different magazines and anthologies, including mystery, science fiction, and mainstream publications. He is the fiction editor of *HazMat Review,* a literary journal, and Director of Programming for Writers & Books, a non-profit literary center in Rochester, New York.

Sean Thomas Dougherty, a former high school dropout and factory worker, is author of six books, including the forthcoming *Nightshift According to Lorca* (MAMMOTH books), *The Biography of Broken Things* (Mitkimitki Press) and *Except by Falling,* winner of 2000 Pinyon Press Poetry Prize from Mesa State College. He teaches at Penn State Erie.

Brian Doyle is the editor of *Portland Magazine* at the University of Portland, and the author of three collections of essays: *Credo, Saints Passionate & Peculiar*, and (with his father Jim Doyle) *Two Voices*.

Denise Duhamel's most recent publications are *Queen for a Day: Selected and New Poems* (University of Pittsburgh, 2001) and *Little Novels* (with Maureen Seaton, Pearl Editions, 2002). She teaches creative writing at Florida International University in Miami.

Janice Eidus, novelist, short story writer, and essayist, has twice won the prestigious O. Henry Prize for her short stories, as well as a Redbook Prize and a Pushcart Prize. She is the author of four highly acclaimed books, *The Celibacy Club, Vito Loves Geraldine, Urban Bliss,* and *Faithful Rebecca*.

Gary Fincke is the Writers' Institute Director at Susquehanna University. His most recent collection of fiction is *Emergency Calls* (Missouri), and he has new stories in *Black Warrior Review, The Idaho Review, Cimarron Review, Flyway,* and *The Journal*.

Sherrie Flick's very short fiction has appeared in *North American Review, Quarterly West, Prairie Schooner, Quarter After Eight,* and elsewhere. Her book length short-short manuscript, *I Call This Flirting,* is currently available for publication. She lives in Pittsburgh, Pennsylvania.

Melissa Fraterrigo's fiction and nonfiction have appeared in *So to Speak, Black Warrior Review, Arts & Letters, Chattahoochee Review,* and other publications. In 2001 she was awarded the Charles B. Wood Award from the Carolina Quarterly for outstanding fiction from an emerging writer. Currently, she teaches English at Penn State Erie.

Sarah Freligh is the author of a chapbook, *Bonus Baby* (Polo Grounds Press, 2000), and has published her poetry and fiction in *The Comstock Review, Iowa Woman, Painted Bride Quarterly, Third Coast, Cimarron Review* and many other journals.

Jamey Gallagher lives in South Jersey. He is currently working on a collection of short stories and recently completed *365 Stories: A Story a Day for a Year* at www.jrnl1.com/365.

Stephen Gibson is the author the story collection, *The Persistence of Memory*, a finalist for the 2001 Flannery O'Connor Prize. Other stories from the collection have appeared in *Five Points, Georgia Review, Southern Review,* and elsewhere. Red Hen Press brought out a collection of Gibson's poetry, *Rorschach Art,* in November 2001.

Molly Giles' latest book is *Iron Shoes*. She directs the writing program at the University of Arkansas.

Michael Griffith's novel, *Spikes*, appeared from Arcade in 2001 and is available in paperback from Arcade/Little-Brown. A collection of stories and a novella, *Bibliophilia*, will be released in 2003. He is an assistant professor at the University of Cincinnati.

Maurice Kilwein Guevara was born in Belencito, Colombia in 1961 and raised in Pittsburgh, Pennsylvania. He is Professor of English at Indiana University of Pennsylvania. His third collection, *Autobiography of So-and-so: Poems in Prose*, came out in 2001 (New Issues Press).

Lola Haskins has published seven books of poetry, most recently *The Rim Benders* (Anhinga, 2001*)*. *Desire Lines: New and Selected Poems* will be published in 2004 by BOA.

Robin Hemley is the author of six books of fiction and nonfiction, most recently *Invented Eden*, forthcoming from FSG in May 2003. His work has been widely anthologized and translated. He teaches creative writing at The University of Utah and directs the low-residency MFA at Vermont College.

William Heyen is glad to be retired from teaching. He recently edited *September 11, 2001: American Writers Respond* (Etruscan Press). Three of his books—*The Rope* (poems), *Home* (essays), and *The Hummingbird Corporation* (stories)—will soon be published by MAMMOTH books.

Jim Heynen's most recent collection of short-shorts, *The Boys House*, was selected as an Editors' Choice 2001 by *Newsday*, *The Bloomsbury Review*, and *Booklist*. The paperback edition was released in July 2002. He is currently writer-in-residence at St. Olaf College in Northfield, Minnesota, and lives in St. Paul.

Brian Hinshaw received an MFA in Creative Writing from Emerson College and now teaches at the University of Wisconsin-Milwaukee and edits the website www.american-lit.com. *The Custodian* comes from a class in Short Short Stories taught by Pamela Painter, and was selected as "The World's Best Short Short Story" for 1996 by *Sundog: The Southeast Review*.

Susan Hubbard's books include *Blue Money*, winner of the Janet Heidinger Kakfa Prize, and *Walking on Ice*, recipient of the Associated Writing Programs' Prize for Short Fiction. Her work has appeared in *TriQuarterly*, *The Mississippi Review*, *and Ploughshares*. She is coeditor of *100% Pure Florida Fiction*, an anthology. Hubbard teaches at the University of Central Florida and serves as President of Associated Writing Programs.

Mary Hussmann received her MFA from The University of Iowa, and teaches at St. Lawrence University. She co-edited *Transgressions: The Iowa Review Anthology of Innovative Fiction*, and has published essays, poetry, reviews and interviews in anthologies and journals including *American Nature Writing 2001*, *The Iowa Review*, *The Kenyon Review*, *Brevity*, and *5Trope*, among others.

Kit Coyne Irwin survived 12 years of Catholic school and being bitten by an orangutan. Though never carried away by a tornado, she has extensive recliner experience. She lives in Massachusetts with her husband Mark, dog Massey, and cats Niles and Frasier.

Jesse Lee Kercheval is the author of six books of poetry, fiction and creative nonfiction and one other short short story, "Carpathia," which appears in the Norton anthology *Micro Fiction*. She teaches at the University of Wisconsin Madison where she directs the Wisconsin Institute for Creative Writing.

Christine Boyka Kluge has received six Pushcart Prize nominations. Her first book is forthcoming from Bitter Oleander Press. *The Bitter Oleander* gave her the 1999 Frances Locke Poetry Award and featured her writing and interview in Fall 2001. Ten poems will appear in an upcoming *Tupelo Press* prose poetry anthology.

Dave Kress lives in Rhode Island. His novel, *Counting Zero*, was published by MAMMOTH books in 1999.

Marilyn Krysl's latest book of stories is *How To Accommodate Men* (Coffee House 1998). Her stories have appeared in *Best American Short Stories 2000, O. Henry Prize Stories,* and the *Pushcart Prize Anthology*. She served as Artist in Residence at the Center for Human Caring, worked for Peace Brigade International in Sri Lanka, and volunteered at Mother Teresa's Kalighat Home for the Destitute and Dying in Calcutta.

Aimee LaBrie graduated from Penn State University with an MFA in Fiction in 2001. Her short stories have appeared in *Quarter After Eight, Beloit Fiction Review, Pleiades, Spelunker Flophouse, Permafrost* and other literary journals.

Gerry LaFemina is the author of several collections of poetry including *Graffiti Heart*, the 2001 Anthony Piccione Award winner in Poetry from MAMMOTH books. "The Dharma of Punk" comes from his collection of prose poems, *Zarathustra in Love*.

Roger Lathbury, born in Paris and Sao Paulo, is the author of several books, including *Wuthering Heights, The American People's Encyclopedia* (Volume 12), and, most recently, *The Iliad*. He lives in Washington, DC, and is married to the former Jefferson Memorial.

Lorraine Lopez's first book, *Soy la Avon Lady and Other Stories* won the inaugural Miguel Marmol Prize for Fiction and was published by Curbstone Press in May 2002. She lives in Nashville where she is an assistant professor of English at Vanderbilt University.

Bret Lott lives in Mt. Pleasant, South Carolina, and teaches at the College of Charleston and Vermont College. He is the author of eight books, including *Jewel, The Hunt Club*, and *The Man Who Owned Vermont*.

Liz Mandrell teaches composition and creative writing at Morehead State University. Her fiction has appeared in *The Georgia Review* and *Libidio*. Her nonfiction has appeared in *Cincinnati* and *Appalachian Heritage*. She lives in Mount Sterling, Kentucky, with her husband, Darrell.

Peter Markus has published over two-hundred other short short fictions from this series in journals such as *Black Warrior Review, Massachusetts Review, Quarterly West, Northwest Review, New Orleans Review, Third Coast, Faultline, LitRag,* as well as on-line at *failbetter, 5_Trope, Pindeldyboz, Drunken Boat, Diagram,* and *Taint.*

Debra Marquart's books include *Everything's a Verb: Poems* (New Rivers Press, 1995), *The Hunger Bone: Rock & Roll Stories* (New Rivers Press, 2001), and a second poetry collection, *From Sweetness* (Pearl Editions, 2002). Marquart is the poetry editor of *Flyway Literary Review* and coordinator of the Creative Writing Program at Iowa State University.

Lee Martin is the author of a novel, *Quakertown;* a memoir, *From Our House;* a story collection, *The Least You Need to Know;* and the essay collection, *Turning Bones,* which is forthcoming from the University of Nebraska Press. He teaches in the MFA Program at The Ohio State University.

Michael Martone was born in Fort Wayne, Indiana, is 47 years old, bats and throws right handed, and has brown eyes and gray hair. *The Blue Guide to Indiana* is his newest book. *The Flatness and Other Landscapes* won the AWP Award for Creative Nonfiction He lives in Tuscaloosa, Alabama.

C.M. Mayo is the author of *Sky Over El Nido,* which won the Flannery O'Connor Award for Short Fiction, and *Miraculous Air: Journey of a Thousand Miles through Baja California, the Other Mexico.* Mayo is founding editor of *Tameme,* the bilingual journal of new writing from Canada, the U.S. and Mexico. Mayo's website is www.cmmayo.com.

Jane McCafferty is author of *Director of The World,* a book of stories, and *One Heart,* a novel. Her stories and essays have been widely published. She enjoyed the challenge of this brevity.

Clint McCown teaches creative writing at Beloit College, where he also edits the *Beloit Fiction Journal.* His books include *Sidetracks, Wind Over Water, The Member-Guest,* and *War Memorials.*

Melissa McCracken writes that she is an itinerant writer slowly working her way West while publishing short-shorts and working on a nonfiction book about her recent brain surgery.

Kathleen McGookey's book of prose poems is *Whatever Shines* (White Pine, 2001). Her work has appeared in over forty journals, including *Cimarron Review, Epoch, Field, The Journal, The Prose Poem: An International Journal,* and *Quarterly West.* Her website is www.kathleenmcgookey.com.

Robert McGovern is an undergraduate student at the Pennsylvania State University. He has poems forthcoming in the journal *Pennsylvania English*.

Corey Messler is the owner of Burke's Book Store, in Memphis, Tennessee, one of the country's oldest (1875) and best independent bookstores. He has published poetry and fiction in numerous journals including *Pindeldyboz, Black Dirt, Thema, Mars Hill Review, Poet Lore*, and others, and his work appears in *New Stories from the South: The Year's Best 2002*, published by Algonquin Books. His first novel, *Talk: A Novel is Dialogue*, came out in 2002 from Livingston Press.

Alyce Miller is the author of a collection of stories, *The Nature of Longing* (winner of the Flannery O'Connor Award), and a novel, *Stopping for Green Lights*. Her essays, poetry, and fiction have appeared in numerous literary magazines. She is a professor of English at Indiana University in Bloomington, and will receive her JD degree from the IU School of Law in spring 2003.

Ben Miller has been compiling a numbered series of texts since 1993. Project segments have appeared in *New Letters, The North American Review, Chicago Review, Western Humanities Review, Northwest Review, Seneca Review, Green Mountains Review, New Orleans Review, American Letters & Commentary* and many others. His awards include a fellowship from the NEA.

Christina Milletti is an Assistant Professor of English at Eastern Michigan University. Her fiction has appeared in several journals and anthologies, most recently Harcourt's *Best New American Voices,* Scribner's *Best of the Fiction Workshops, The Greensboro Review,* and *The Chicago Review.* She has written a collection of short stories, *The Religious*, and is at work on a novel, *Room in the Hotel America.*

Gwendolyn Joyce Mintz is a former news writer and college instructor. She currently writes full-time, poetry as well as fiction.

Dinty W. Moore is the author of *Toothpick Men* and *The Accidental Buddhist.* He has written for *Salon, The New York Times Magazine, Utne Reader, Crazyhorse, Arts & Letters,* and numerous other magazines and journals. He was once shoved onto the floor by Richard Nixon's press secretary.

Kirk Nesset's stories and poems have appeared lately in *The Paris Review, Ploughshares, Raritan, Gettysburg Review, Iowa Review, Boston Review, Prairie Schooner,* and elsewhere. He is author of a nonfiction study, *The Stories of Raymond Carver,* published by Ohio University Press. He teaches Literature and Creative Writing at Allegheny College.

Josip Novakovich teaches at Penn State. His collection of stories, *Salvation and Other Disasters,* won an American Book Award from the Before Columbus Foundation and a Whiting Award. *TriQuarterly Press* will publish his new novel and *White Pine* his new collection of essays.

Pamela Painter is the author of two story collections, *Getting To Know the Weather* and *The Long and Short of It*. She is also co-author of *What If? Writing Exercises For Fiction Writers*. Her stories have appeared in *The Atlantic, Harper's, Kenyon Review*, and *Ploughshares*, among others. Painter lives in Boston and teaches at Emerson College.

Anne Panning has published a book of stories, *The Price of Eggs*, as well as stories and essays in places such as *Prairie Schooner, Beloit Fiction Journal, New Letters, The Bellingham Review, The South Dakota Review, The Black Warrior Review*, and others. Her novel manuscript, *Carrot Lake, Carrot Cake*, just won the Hackney Award for the Novel. She lives in Brockport, New York.

Richard Pearse is a professor of English at Brooklyn College. His stories and poems have been published in *The Paris Review, Prairie Schooner, Fiction*, and many other journals. He has five collections of poetry, and last year Rattapallax Press issued his *Private Drives: Selected Poems*, 1969-2001.

Susan Perabo is Writer in Residence and Associate Professor of English at Dickinson College. Her collection of short stories, *Who I Was Supposed to Be*, and her first novel, *The Broken Places*, were published by Simon & Schuster.

Ben Percy is a MFA candidate at Southern Illinois University whose work has appeared in *The Mississippi Review, The Florida Review, The Oyster Boy Review*, and other journals. He recently received the runner-up prize for *The Chicago Tribune's* Nelson Algren Award and is at work on a novel.

Wendy Ring has published short shorts in *The North American Review, Sun Dog: The Southeast Review*, and the anthology *Micro Fiction*. She hopes to finish a collection of stories shortly.

Josh Russell's very short stories have appeared in *Epoch, Paragraph, Quarterly West, Sundog, Antioch, Black Warrior, Carolina, Colorado* and *Mid-American* reviews, and an Oat City Press limited edition, *Winter on Fifth Avenue, New York*. His novel is *Yellow Jack* (W. W. Norton). He lives in New Orleans and teaches at Tulane University.

Scott Russell Sanders is the author of eighteen books, including *Staying Put, Hunting for Hope*, and *The Force of Spirit*. His writing has been honored by the PEN Syndicated Fiction Award, the John Burroughs Essay Award, and the Lannan Literary Award. He is Distinguished Professor of English at Indiana University in the hardwood hill country of the White River Valley.

Geoff Schmidt is an Assistant Professor of English at Southern Illinois University at Edwardsville. His first novel, *Write Your Heart Out: Advice from the Moon Winx Motel*, was published in 2000 by Smallmouth Press.

Davis Schneiderman's creative work was nominated for a 2001 Pushcart Prize and has been accepted by *Exquisite Corpse, The Iowa Review Web, Quarter*

After Eight, The Little Magazine, Happy, Gargoyle, EnterText, 3AM Magazine, and *The Café Irreal,* among others.

Keith Scribner's novel, *The GoodLife,* was published by Riverhead Books (Penguin Putnam) in 1999; his second novel, *Miracle Girl,* will be published by Riverhead Books in 2003. Shorter work has appeared in journals such as *American Short Fiction* and *Quarterly West.* He teaches in the MFA program at Oregon State University.

Jeremy Sellers is an English major at Penn State Altoona and serves as Executive Editor of *Hard Freight,* Penn State Altoona's Magazine of the Literary and Visual Arts. He graduated from the same high school as the novelist Dean R. Koontz.

Tyson Sharbaugh is from Baltimore, Maryland, and is studying communications at Penn State. He hopes to become a successful screenwriter but also enjoys writing short fiction. If he had any interesting hobbies or accomplishments, he could list them here, but since he doesn't, he can't.

Steven Sherrill teaches at Penn State Altoona. He is the recipient of a 2002 NEA Fiction Fellowship. His first novel, *The Minotaur Takes a Cigarette Break,* was reprinted by Picador USA in November 2002 and by Canongate UK in 2003. His work has appeared in *Best American Poetry, Kenyon Review, River Styx, The Georgia Review,* and others.

Barry Silesky is author of *One Thing That Can Save Us* (Coffee House Press) and many shorts in various magazines—*Fiction, Fiction International, The Best Of The Prose Poem, Boulevard,* etc. He is editor of the literary journal *ACM* and has also written biographies of Lawrence Ferlinghetti (Warner Books) and John Gardner (Algonquin Books).

Natalia Rachel Singer's short fiction has appeared in *Sundog, Rhino,* and the anthology of short shorts, *Microfiction* (Norton, 1996) edited by Jerome Stern. She has won first prize in the World's Best Short Short Story Contest, sponsored by Florida State University, and has been a frequent finalist. She is an associate professor of English at St. Lawrence University.

Brent Spencer is the author of *Are We Not Men?* (Arcade, 1996) and *The Lost Son* (Arcade, 1995). He teaches creative writing at Creighton University in Omaha. His fiction has appeared in *Glimmer Train, The Atlantic Monthly, The Antioch Review, The American Literary Review, The Missouri Review, GQ,* and elsewhere.

Lori Ann Stephens teaches a short story course at University of Texas at Dallas, where she is completing her Ph.D. in Aesthetic Studies. She resides in Richardson, Texas, with her son, Trevor. She still seeks creative advice from her first creative writing teacher and friend, Robert Nelsen.

J. David Stevens teaches creative writing at Seton Hall University in New Jersey. His latest stories appear in *Harper's*, *The Paris Review*, *Mid-American Review*, and *Carolina Quarterly*.

Julie Stotz-Ghosh is a graduate of Western Michigan University's MFA and Ph.D. programs in creative writing and has published poetry and nonfiction in anthologies and journals such as *Third Coast*, *I-94*, and *Encore*.

Virgil Suarez was born in Havana, Cuba. He has lived in the United States since 1974. He is the author and editor of over 20 books. Most recently he has published the poetry collections *Banyan* (LSU Press), *Palm Crows* (University of Arizona Press) and *Guide to the Blue Tongue* (Illinois Poetry Series). He teaches creative writing at Florida State University and lives mostly in Miami.

Philip Terman was born in Cleveland, Ohio. His collections of poems include *What Survives* (Sow's Ear Press Chapbook Award) and *The House of Sages* (MAMMOTH books). A new collection, *Book of the Unbroken Days*, will appear in 2003. He is editing a collection of essays on the poet James Wright.

Wayne Thomas studies creative writing in the MFA program at Georgia College & State University and serves as Assistant Editor of *Arts & Letters: Journal of Contemporary Culture*. His interview with playwright John Guare appeared in the Spring 2003 *Arts & Letters*.

Melanie Rae Thon is the author of the novels *Sweet Hearts*, *Meteors in August* and *Iona Moon* and the story collections *First, Body* and *Girls in the Grass*. Her work has appeared in *Paris Review*, *Story*, *Granta*, and *Best American Short Stories*.

Anthony Tognazzi's work has appeared in *Quarterly West*, *paragraph*, *Quick Fiction*, and *The Alaska Quarterly Review*. He has received a Louis Davidson Ellis Literary Award for fiction, an Academy of American Poets Prize, an AWP award and a Ledig House Fellowship. He is originally from California.

Pam Ullman lives and writes in Shillington, Pennsylvania. Her short fiction has appeared on the Random House *Bold Type* website, in such journals as *Lynx Eye*, *The Dickinson Review*, and *The White Wall Review*, and in *Love is Ageless* (Lompico Creek Press), an anthology of poetry and stories about Alzheimer's disease.

Antonio Vallone is an associate professor of English at Penn State DuBois. His books of poetry include *The Blackbirds' Applause*, *Grass Saxophones*, *Golden Carp*, *Chinese Bats,* and *American Zen*.

Sharon Wahl is writing a book of love stories based on philosophy texts. She has published stories, poems, and reviews in the *Chicago Tribune*, *The Iowa Review*, and many other journals. She teaches at the University of Phoenix and will be the Emerging Writer in Residence at Penn State Altoona in 2003.

Ron Wallace is the author of eleven books of poetry, fiction, and criticism, including *Long for This World: New & Selected Poems* (University of Pittsburgh Press, 2003) and *Quick Bright Things: Stories* (Mid-List Press, 2000). He is co-director of the creative writing program at the University of Wisconsin-Madison and editor of the University of Wisconsin Press poetry series.

Michael Waters teaches at Salisbury University on the Eastern Shore of Maryland. He has published seven volumes of poetry, including *Bountiful* (Carnegie Mellon, 1992), *Green Ash, Red Maple, Black Gum* (BOA Editions, 1997), and *Parthenopi: New and Selected Poems* (BOA Editions, 2001), and has co-edited *Contemporary American Poetry* (Houghton Mifflin, 2001) and *Perfect in Their Art: Poems on Boxing from Homer to Ali* (Southern Illinois UP, 2003).

Gabriel Welsch is a former landscape designer whose short stories appear in *Mid-American Review, Cream City Review, Antietam Review, Beloit Fiction Journal, Quarter After Eight, Flint Hills Review,* and several other journals. In 2002, he won the Thoreau Residency at the Toledo Botanical Gardens, awarded by *Mid-American Review*.

Allen Woodman directs the creative writing program at Northern Arizona University. He is the author of *Saved by Mr. F. Scott Fitzgerald,* a collection of humorous stories for adults, and co-author of *The Cows Are Going to Paris,* a children's picture book.

Angus Woodward's fiction, poetry, and nonfiction have appeared in *Iowa Review, Writer's Chronicle, Rhino, Laurel Review, Prairie Schooner, Pennsylvania English, Talking River Review,* and several others. He lives and works in Baton Rouge.

Ronder Thomas Young has published the novels *Learning by Heart, Moving Mama to Town,* and *Objects in Mirror* as well as numerous short stories and essays. She lives in Norcross, Georgia with her husband and three sons.

 **PERMISSIONS**

"Three Legged Dogs" by Jane Armstrong reprinted from *Beloit Fiction Journal* Spring 1992, with permission of the author.

"In the Middle" by Michael A. Arnzen reprinted from *Insolent Rudder*, September 2002, with permission of the author.

"Broke" by Aimee Bender is reprinted with permission of the author.

"Hugh of Provo" by Tom Bradley reprinted from *RealPoetik 2000* with permission of the author.

"The Dark Side of the Moon" by Mark Budman reprinted from *In Posse*, Issue 5, May 2000, with permission of the author.

"Bouncing" by Keith Loren Carter reprinted from *Mid-American Review*, Volume XXII, Number 2, with permission of the author.

"Excuses I Have Already Used" by Antonia Clark reprinted from *StoryQuarterly*, #33, 1997, with permission of the author.

"Reading Group Discussion Guide" by Denise Duhamel reprinted by permission of the author.

"Another Thing" by Sarah Freligh reprinted from *Painted Bride Quarterly* No. 59 with permission of the author.

"Back" by Sherrie Flick reprinted from *Quarterly West*, Issue #45 with permission of the author.

"Hermit Crab" by Stephen Gibson reprinted from *Fiction*, Vol.11, No. 2, 1993, with permission of the author.

"Protest" by Molly Giles reprinted from *Blue Mesa Review*, 14, with permission of the author.

"Bad Slaw, Bad Karma, Badass" and "Dissonant, Hurtful, and Hers" by Michael Griffith reprinted from *Connecticut Review* with permission of the author.

"Ste. Francoise des Croissants" by Lola Haskins was published in *Green Mountains Review*. Reprinted with permission of the author.

"Why Would a Woman Pour Boiling Water on her Head?" by Jim Heynen reprinted from *Why Would A Woman Pour Boiling Water on her Head?,* Tribolite

Press, Denton, Texas, 2001, copyright Jim Heynen, with permission of the author.

"The Custodian" by Brian Hinshaw reprinted from *Sundog: The Southeast Review*, Vol. 16, No. 2, with permission of the author.

"Psychic Takes a Greyhound" by Susan Hubbard reprinted from *America West* (Jan. 1997) with permission of the author.

"Under Glass" by Susan Hubbard reprinted from *Blue Money* (University of Missouri Press, 1999) with permission of the author.

"After the Funeral, Joe Tells a Story" by Jesse Lee Kercheval appears with permission of the author.

"Steeplejack" by Jesse Lee Kercheval is reprinted from *Crazyhorse* 61 (2002) with permission of the author.

"Grimm the Janitor" and "Fast Forward" by Maurice Kilwein Guevara reprinted from *Autobiography of So-and-So*, New Issues Press, 2001, with permission of the author and the publisher.

"Cold Truth, Bright as a Coin" by Christine Boyka Kluge reprinted from *The Bitter Oleander*, Spring 2001, with permission of the author.

"Encore" by Aimee LaBrie reprinted from *Quarter After Eight* with permission of the author.

"The Dharma of Punk" by Gerry LaFemina reprinted from *Zarathustra in Love*, Mayapple Press, 2001, by permission of the author.

"Girl" by Peter Markus reprinted from *Barnabe Mountain Review* #4, with permission of the author.

"Girl is a River" by Peter Markus, reprinted from *Flyway*, Spring/Fall 2001, with permission of the author.

"What We Do With The Fish After We Gut The Fish" by Peter Markus reprinted from *New Orleans Review*, Volume 25, Number 4, with permission of the author.

"Dylan's Lost Years" and "This New Quiet" by Debra Marquart reprinted from *The Hunger Bone: Rock & Roll Stories*, New Rivers Press, 2001 with permission of the author.

"From the Torre Latino" by C.M. Mayo was previously published in a slightly different form in *Permafrost*, No. 22. Reprinted with permission of the author.

"Implosion" by Melissa McCracken reprinted from *New Letters*, University of Missouri, Kansas City, 2000, Vol. 67, 1 with permission of the author.

"It Would've Been Hot" by Melissa McCracken reprinted from *Stray Dog 2*, Prilly & Tru Publications, Inc., 2002 with permission of the author.

"Weathering" by Gwendolyn Joyce Mintz originally appeared in *Puerto del Sol*, Spring 1991, Vol. 29 (1). Reprinted by permission of the author.

"Nicaragua" by Kirk Nesset reprinted from *Fiction*, Winter 2002/2003, with permission of the author.

"Ladybug Inn" by Kirk Nesset reprinted from *Witness*, Spring 2003, with permission of the author.

"God" by Pamela Painter reprinted from *StoryQuarterly* 34, by permission of the author.

"The New Year" by Pamela Painter reprinted from *The Long and Short of It*, Carnegie Mellon University Press, 1999 with permission of the author.

"Cat Custody" by Richard Pearse, reprinted from *Quick Fiction*, Issue One, May 2002, with permission of the author.

"Black Cat" by Josh Russell reprinted from *Sundog: The Southeast Quarterly*, Vol. 18, No. 2, Summer 1998 with permission of the author.

"Winter on Fifth Avenue, New York" by Josh Russell reprinted from the *Oat City Press* limited edition *Winter on Fifth Avenue, New York* and from *The Antioch Review*, Vol. 57, No. 1, Winter 1999 with permission of the author.

"Rocket Science" by Wendy Ring reprinted from *The North American Review*, May/August 1999, with permission of the author.

"Love-Crossed Carpenter" and "The Multiplication of Wool" by Scott Russell Sanders reprinted from *Wilderness Plots* (Morrow, 1983; Ohio State UP, 1988) with permission of the author.

"The Killer Clowns" by Barry Silesky was first published in *Fiction*, Vol. 11, #3, City Univ. of New York. Reprinted by permission of the author.

"Goatboy Considers Winter" by Natalia Rachel Singer reprinted from *Sundog: The Southeast Review*, Volume 15/16, Number 2/1, fall, 1996, by permission of the author.

"Sultan" by Natalia Rachel Singer reprinted from *Rhino 2000*, by permission of the author.